KRUPP'S LULU

ALSO BY GORDON LISH

KRUPP'S LULU

Gordon Lish

STORIES

FOUR WALLS EIGHT WINDOWS
NEW YORK / LONDON

© 2000 BY GORDON LISH

PUBLISHED IN THE UNITED STATES BY
FOUR WALLS EIGHT WINDOWS
39 WEST 14TH STREET
NEW YORK, N.Y. 10011
HTTP://WWW.FOURWALLSEIGHTWINDOWS.COM

U.K. OFFICES:
FOUR WALLS EIGHT WINDOWS/TURNAROUND
UNIT 3 OLYMPIA TRADING ESTATE
COBURG ROAD, WOOD GREEN
LONDON N22 6Z

FIRST PRINTING MARCH 2000.

LIBRARY OF CONGRESS CATALOGUING-IN-PUBLICATION DATA:
LISH, GORDON
KRUPP'S LULU: STORIES / GORDON LISH
P. CM.
ISBN 1-56858-154-8
I. TITLE.
PS3562.I74K78   2000
813'.54—DC21   99-086329
CIP

PRINTED IN THE UNITED STATES
TEXT DESIGN BY INK, INC.
PRODUCTION BY MORGAN BRILLIANT
10 9 8 7 6 5 4 3 2 1

FOR ROBERT BOYERS,
PLACE–MAKER, ROOM–MAKER, MENSCH

AND TO JANE
DANA
CYNTHIA
MORGAN
KATHRYN
JILLELLYN
CAROLYN
NIKKI
JONN
KATHY
BONITA
KATHERINE
MARGERY
PATTY
SUZANNE
JAN

AND FOR ROSIE THE ROSIEST,
FOR NINA HERSELF ROSENWALD,
TUMELER, ENABLER, ANCHORAGE

To obey the word is to proceed murder by murder.

—EDMOND JABÈS

This world—oh, you know it!

—F. W. NIETZSCHE

A white horse is not a horse.

—ANCIENT MAXIM

CONTENTS

KRUPP'S LULU

FACTS OF STEEL

NOTHING WOULD PLEASE ME more than for me as an artist to be free to sit here and tell you the truth. But they won't let me do it. May I tell you something? They will not let me do it. The whole kit and caboodle of them are all in cahoots. I'm telling you, it sickens me, it just sickens me, the way things are. You cry out against it from the pit of despair, but ask yourself, does it do any good? This is why I have no choice but to resort to ruse after ruse. God knows I get no pleasure from it. The last thing I as an artist desire is for me to have to sit here and keep developing this worldwide rep I have as a rusefier extraordinaire. But am I the one who has the say? I am not the one who has the say. You heard of the road of life? Because this is exactly what this is, it is the fucking road of life. Oh, how could I have been such a fool, thinking to myself Gordon darling you are an artist darling you are in the driver's seat darling there will cometh your day in the sun. But who are they giving any day in the sun? They are not giving anybody any day in the sun. So you see how come the facts of steel? Ergo, the facts of steel. Can I tell you something? Let me tell you something. Whatever your occupational pursuit, take pains you throw the devils off. Because it's either that or you're under their thumb. You have heard of the proverbial thumb? Because it's either they get you under it or they bind you hand and foot. But save your tears. Nobody cares. Believe me, they can't wait to stand there and spit in your face. The whole mob of them, once they get their hooks into you, your goose is cooked. I'm sorry, but they're worse than Greeks. Will they let you live? They will not let you live. Will they let you speak? They will not let you speak. And guess who the loser is. Do I have to tell you who the loser is? Because the answer is Mr. and Mrs. John Q. Public. Hey, you're just lucky they don't make you make it zinc. So what chance do I as an artist have but to dance to their tune? You know what it is? I'm telling you what it is. It is a national disgrace. But I Gordon did not start it. It was either Andrew Carnegie who did or the other cocksucker, Henry James.

GROUND

YOU EVER PLAY THE GAME which when you were little of you take your fingers and you walk the feet of them all around? Not all around anywhere, not walk the feet of them all around just anywhere, but walking them just on the rug your hand was on or on the bed your hand was on or on something you could be on if you put your hand down like fingers are feet like that on it—like even like on a table?

So you ever play it, this game?

He was a little man.

If you were me, then he was a little man.

But even if you were a little girl, then maybe he was still a little man.

And strong.

Strong and could do anything.

Mine could fly if I got a piece of tissue paper or if I tore off a piece of something else like that like some type of paper like that and got it caught or got it stuck up in between the tops of them—my fingers, my fingers!—kept it caught in there and stuck in there up there where the head was—like these ones here, like the tops of these ones two ones here—can't you see where these ones two ones here, how they come together as fingers where there's this crease in them, you could call it, or call it, you know, like this crease?

It was the head.

The crease was the head—and the rest was the arms and the legs—and the tips of the fingers, like call them the fingertips, they were the feet—and wait a minute, wait a minute—the piece of the tissue paper or the piece of any other kind of paper, it was the cape the little man had coming out of the back of his head, it was the cape which the little man had on him for him to have on him like a flying cape for the little man to stand there on his feet and have it flung out back behind him from out in the back of his head for when the little man wanted to go ahead and jump up and fly anywhere up over something so long as there was room in the air up over whatever it was, which was where the air was.

But I outgrew the flying idea.

I'm sitting here telling you I went ahead and decided in my mind for me to go ahead and outgrow the whole idea of the little man flying anywhere as being like too much of a magic idea.

I got old enough—probably seven, probably eight— where it was an age I was in in which I did not like it anymore as far as the whole idea of me letting the little man fly up into the air over anything, or even just the idea of just me letting the little man take off up into the air for only like a little bit from like the rug, let us say, or like from maybe, in a pinch, from like just the back of my other hand.

Flying, if you went ahead and had the flying in the

game, then face facts, face facts, since when was it with anything in the game like flying like that in it still even in any sense of the word still a game?

I don't think, or didn't think, it was anything.

Flying—Jesus.

Come on, don't make me laugh, flying, ha ha.

Because it was only a game when it was the way it first was when you first started to play it, the little man walking all around everywhere in more or less in the same place.

Or skipping if he wanted.

Or running if he wanted.

Or just like standing there and not moving if standing there and not moving was what the little man felt like doing for the time being.

Or even falling down on your knuckles and making believe it was his knees.

It had to be a game.

It had to be in a place.

He could jump, the little man could jump, it was still okay as a game if, okay, if the little man jumped, but the whole idea of it was the little man had to end up coming back down onto whichever it was your hand was on—like some rug and so on, or like some bed and so on, like even on just like this one particular place they had in your house so long as it was clear to you right from the start in your mind like this one particular place the little man is starting out from is the little man's place for the time being.

But letting the little man fly, no, Jesus Christ, no, wasn't flying for fucking babies?

I got rid of it.

I threw it away.

Did it probably around the age, I bet, of six probably or of seven, it could have been, or maybe even as late as maybe the age of eight.

The tissue, I mean.

Or it could have just been not just tissue in the sense of tissue paper but tissue in the sense of something which was paper like tissue paper.

But the place we had, my family, the place we had, it always had tissue paper put away in it somewhere away in it back in those old, you know, back in those old or call them olden days.

This place I live in now, there is no tissue paper around in it anywhere, except for toilet paper.

But neither is there any little boy or little girl in it who's constantly asking you for anything.

Those were the days!

God, I miss those old or olden days.

There was this one place which when you, where when you really set your mind to it, it made the best place for me to play the game of the little man with or without his cape of tissue paper on him.

Do you call it a throw?

I think they call it a throw.

It was on the floor all of the time in our parlor all of the time—which had these stones in all of these different colors—but so was the throw, wasn't it?

All colors?

In different-colored colors?

In all of these various different-colored colors?

I don't know.

It was made out of old socks or something—or out of old, you know, old stockings.

Maybe it was old rags it was made out of.

I could play for hours.

I could get him down there on this throw thing which they had in there in the parlor and keep him going in there with me for hours, the little man.

Walking mostly.

Mostly walking mostly.

But skipping when he had this skipping feeling in him arising in him in this mind in him that, you know, that he wanted, as the little man, to skip. Or go skipping.

Or jump, for instance.

Maybe run maybe if he wanted.

You know.

It was up to him, the little man.

It was all of it always all of it up only to him.

Did I tell you the fringe was the thing?

It had this fringe—the throw on the floor in the parlor, it had like this fringe on it sticking out from it in the sense of like a fringe on it, which was definitely, as far as me, the thing.

The little man getting to the edge of the throw and then making up his mind as far as the fringe.

Him getting there to the edge of it and like making up his mind what to do, what to do?—what do I do, what do I do?—do I step off and get myself down into it in the fringe where there are all of these like, my God, like cords cut off?—where there are down there like these big dirty cut-off cords cut off?—like in Jesus fucking Christ, the fringe!

Scatter—there's the word for us, my God, that's the word for it!—scatter, isn't it scatter?

It wasn't a throw they said it was—it was a scatter which they said it was.

You know, the rug.

A scatter rug.

Fringed.

Like made of tied-together knots of things—like of socks and things—a stocking where there wasn't anymore socks to go with it anymore—and all around the edge all around it, this cut-off dirty-looking stuff.

Fringe.

But oh, the colors of it, the colors of it, oh!—and the

same went for, and the same was always going for the stones where when I went there to the parlor there was the floor for me to get down on and as a boy be happy forever and play.

Oh, play.

All the time never being able for me to wait to get home and then for me to go over there to it in the parlor for it and get him down on it and start us letting him see what the story was going to turn out to be once we got him going as far as the game.

Namely, where he'd go.

Or if he would.

How far he was going to go for him to get anywhere.

And what he'd do if he did.

Sometimes the little man had all of these millions and millions of various different plans he was always thinking about—take a trip here, take a trip there—skip all of the way on the way, jump every other step, or like just keep running like mad.

But you know what?

Mostly the little man just did what he did without him having even any conceivable idea.

But then—whoops!

Uh-oh.

He'd like, you know, he'd like get to the edge.

The older I got, the more and more the little man just went ahead and did that—took a trip and took himself all of the way over to someplace where he was standing right the fuck on it—not the edge of any throw, of course, but the edge, let's call it, of the scatter, I mean!—and then the next thing, it had to be what?—step down into it or don't do anything or go back and make another safer plan or a plan that was safe.

Hey, I tell you it was forever?

The floor all over the parlor, if you were the little man, it looked to you like, hey, that out there, isn't it, if you really look at it, forever out there?

From where you were to all of the way forever?

From all of the stones from under the fringe out to the end of the place where we lived to the whole other rest of everything.

Once you went ahead and took the first step.

Like if you were the little man.

Sun porch, sun porch!

Did I say parlor?

I'm sorry.

Sorry, sorry, sorry, sorry.

The Lishes did not have any parlor.

It had a sun porch over on one side of it—that's what we had, that's what the place we had had!—oh so forever sunny in the sun porch so long as you were never in it without the little man.

Hey, so long as you were never in it without these two ones of your two fingers right up to this crease between them right here.

The place had a sun porch on it and the floor of the sun porch had all of these different-colored field stones on it and the name of the kind of the rug on it, it was named, I'm telling you, a scatter rug, everybody everywhere was always calling it the scatter rug on the floor of the sun porch in the sun porch of where we lived and believe you me when I tell you there were these tied socks and things it was made of, there were like these stockings knotted among the things this thing was actually knotted of, washrags, washrags, pajama legs, nighties, all of it all torn up and all probably all knotted up or probably all tied up but with like these cords of this cut-off crap of it all around all the whole edge of it, and filthy? I'm telling you, it was so filthy and so sickening, but didn't I, Gordon, didn't I get down there and make him be there—him?

These fingers here.

Standing capeless on incomparable feet.

Oh, play, indomitable child, play!

Till they call and call please.

But who hears please?

Nobody hears please—nor needs to.

Hear instead elsewhere, hear instead anywhere—hear instead turn, my beloved, turn!

But the little man never once did.

THIS SIDE OF THE ANIMAL,
OR,
BRICOLAGE

ALL DAY LONG THE MAN READ to them from the storybooks they had. They seemed to like to hear him read to them, but it was not possible for the man to tell if this was truly so. Perhaps they merely put up with the man, his thin white hair hanging in meager clots from his thin glittery skull. Perhaps he had beguiled the children into their feeling sorry for him, or feeling sad for him, or feeling afraid to be unquiet in his company.

The man was so tired.

It hurt his legs when there was one of them, or two, who would take to his wasted lap for a while. But didn't all the parts of the man hurt, no matter if his lap were filled or not with any child?

How on earth had he got this weak, this old?

It had never been his plan. His plan had been to be strong, and to come to the last of his life with the power of his youth. Not one jot of himself would time ever wrest from his fisted hands. But time had, hadn't it?

It was a trick.

It had to have happened when his attention had been situated elsewhere. But where? Certainly not on the children who had conducted into his life these numberless offspring of theirs. There were so many of them—grandchildren, everywhere grandchildren—whereas it required no numbering for the man to reckon there was hardly even one of him and that not at all long from now would there be a sign of even one?

He was alone, had always been alone, and would die—perhaps this very night—as solitary as he had forever in his memory been.

The man had no complaints, not a one.

Yet what could have made him so horribly weary just this very instant?

Fatigue must have hurtled down at him from somewhere overhead and now, at the end of the day, it felt to the man as if exhaustion, breathless itself, lay gasping as it hung from his neck, snatching at the frail struts of the crazed skeleton as the man struggled to free himself from this last cruel assailant.

But why bother?

After all, was the man not preparing for sleep?

They had made up some sort of contraption for him in the main room. It had rather surprised him to turn away from the kisses goodnight and discover behind himself the site where he had sat from sun-up wearing himself out enunciating for the children—for the grandchildren—transformed into what would be his bed. When had this happened? How could it have? Hadn't he been occupying the very place, reading and reading to half of creation since the very stroke of day?

Everyone seemed so capable nowadays.

By what means had this occurred? Was there any precedent in their lives for this? Where was the example in managing matters that had guided these children of his in their accomplishment of such infernal displays of competence, competence—skill and grace? It had not been their mother, surely. Long gone in her dishevelment somewhere to the dreadful margins, hadn't the woman made a proper mess of things, starting with—let gentility select our diction—the exercise, first and last, of, shame, shame, bed-making?

Wait a bit.

He had packed his sleeping pills—but exactly where? The little overnight bag he had fitted them into, what had the children—or the grandchildren, damn every squirming living one of them!—done with it?

Ah, there.

Or here.

Yes, yes.

Just where it ought to be—at the foot—or is it the head?—of this exasperating business that must have once been a couch before the new ingenuity on the march in the world decided to interfere with it.

Well, it wasn't out in the open enough, was it? How come people don't appreciate the courtesy of leaving things where you cannot miss them! Why does it have to be his fault if everything's not where fair play would indicate it be?

He sucked and sucked and accumulated saliva in his mouth and swallowed it waterless—bitter pill, so terrible for such a tiny thing.

His fingers—were the bones breaking?

Not just canny and capable, but thoughtful, actually incomparably thoughtful, once you gave it some thought and actually really thought about it, this family of his, even if none of them knew somebody's overnight bag belonged where a person did not have to spend half his life in a wild hunt for it. Such a fund of solicitude, whatever source it had, it could never be alleged any trace of it could be tied to him. No, it was not that the man did not wish to be generous with himself when called upon to do so. It was rather that the man noticed not all that much of what was available to notice, so that such a call, made however close to the man's ear, might go unattended even when the caller shrieked. But what little the man did attend would grip his attention with a violence that was unrelenting and even eerie. Oh, no, never think the man was not all too excruciatingly aware of what he deigned to be aware of—torn spines of storybooks irksome in their haphazard stacks, toys luridly expressed in polyurethane deep-banked for the night up against the baseboards, frame after frame of family snapshots gaping in disorderly array from every level of tabletop, everywhere the walls flapping with sheets of crayoned and penciled foolscap, none of it had the man elected to ignore—given the chance, he would have discarded the lot, and with gusto!—not least the photograph of the children's mother—was this person a grandmother, in fact?—that now came plunging into view at the far side of the man's pillow and, with it, the career of the marriage, a contending whose vehemence never flagged and whose object was the vector of the slant— upwards versus downwards, downwards versus upwards— of the venetian blinds distributed throughout the dwelling in receipt of the—up to that point—happy couple.

If the woman aimed the slats one way, the man would restore their alignment to the prior disposition. Where the woman had visited would have the arrangement of the window treatment, however maddening the task to effect the detail, reversed upon the man's replacing the woman there.

Oh, it was endless, endless.

Until it ended.

And what had it all had to do with—what?

Neither the man nor the woman might ever have said—unless it had been the use to be made of sunlight if sunlight was in the moment given—or, at all events, by those who paid attention, promised.

Well, it seemed to the man it must have had.

One wanted a radiance either to ignite the ceiling or, otherwise, set fire to the floor.

Make much of what was above.

Make no less of that below.

You choose.

They chose.

Or, rather to say, one of them chose and the other, in a word, unchose. Oh, and speaking of which, never a word was spoken on this score. Sentiments inspiring the impasse dividing him from her and her from him never acquired the status of speech.

Mm, the aphonia of matrimony.

Compromise between the combatants was as impossible as was acknowledgment that each was pledged to oppose the other in a style of disputation unique in the common experience. Any reference to their differences not carried out in silence, would it not prove—talk, talk—the reigning feature in the loser's defeat? Well, there was no backing down, and the man never backed down. Not that the woman ever did, either—there looking him now full in his face, her furious countenance singling out the father of her children as with all his might the man pushed the pillow from the bed so that, in the morning, he would not have to come fighting his way up from the waters of the night with what was left of him—his neck, Christ, the neck—more punished than was necessary.

Wait again, wait!

Was there to be this remembrance of the grandmother and none of the grandfather? Among all these damn pictures, was there honor being paid to the bitch and none, by thunder, to the man!

He got to his feet.

It made him dizzy for him to do it.

And his knees, Jesus!

The pill—good, good—soon, soon—another minute or so and he will have searched the room and determined the worst and then come back to this device to be just in time for the blessing of oblivion.

Nothing, he found nothing, not a hint of himself was there anywhere to be found, not even in settings where a family grouping constituted the topic to be developed within the frame.

Where was he?

Was the man nowhere at all?

He staggered from footing to footing, very nearly falling into things a time or two, before finding—the thing exhibited well back on a tabletop so that evidence of the man's existence might have very nearly persisted in keeping itself hidden from all—before coming across the boy sitting astride the door-to-door photographer's droopy-looking, ruined-looking, condemned-looking pony, naked leg, pale anklet, toe of the dark shoe visible from within the enormous-looking stirrup it was, on this side of the animal, possible for the observer to see.

Oh, what a child!

The child smiled genuinely, genuinely, wonderfully, wonderfully, and the man, feeling himself summoned as all the day long he had not once been, smiled with all his heart right back.

Genuinely, genuinely, except, one supposes, not so wonderfully, wonderfully.

But all right, then!

Then here he was, then, wasn't he!

Wasn't this, then, he, him, the boy that was the man?

The man tried sliding his feet along the floor in order that he might get himself safely home to bed—and there to narratives his nature would hasten to confect for him once the sedative had delivered him all to sleep.

To dreams and dreams and more.

Well, in one there was the woman.

She shrieked at him and shrieked, "Yes, yes, but which way, which? Can't you tell me which?"

In another there was the woman.

But it was not the woman who kept screaming in it at him, "Yoo-hoo, yoo-hoo, thief!—the uses you make of everything and of all the different things!"

Then there was the dream without people.

It was made all of words.

The thing to do in it was to contrive irritating alliterations—yet there was no agency in it doing it.

No woman, no man.

Deficit notwithstanding—no, despite the deficit!—the work indeed was done.

THE POSITIONS

FORGET YOUR DRUGS.

Forget your fucking.

Forget your fancy foods and your ham and eggs and your bacon and eggs and your, you know, your eggs with sausages with on the side your home fries on the side and it's when the eggs are fried and they're fried in the style of frying which is referred to as your eggs fried eggs over easy and they're dished up to you, the eggs are dished up to you with this whole extra thing of extra bacon on the plate and on a plate next to the plate there's these slices of toast buttered with butter on the plate and there's also on the side a milk shake on the side or, okay, let's not say there's a milk shake on the side but just a glass of just milk on the side and the milk's made up of the creamy part of the milk which got itself poured off from the neck of the bottle before anybody could get to the neck of the bottle before it was you who you got to the neck of the bottle and got it all poured off—the creamy part—all for yourself.

So are you listening?

Because I am telling you what the best thing in my life has been to me. You want to know what the best thing in my life has been to me? Because I am telling you, because I am going to tell you what the best thing in my life has been to me.

But before I go ahead and tell you, guess what.

Because no, because what it has not been to me is, no,

it has not been fucking to me and it has not been drugs to me and it has not been going to the movies or been eating franks or been eating franks with sauerkraut on them or with the mustard they used to give you for you to put on the plate next to the franks or for you to put on the plate between the franks back when I was a kid.

Nor been having kids.

Nor been playing with the kids I had.

Nor with the kids which anybody had.

Plus neither shortstop nor pitcher.

It's not been playing the positions of either of them when I played the positions of either of shortstop or of pitcher and was always eating my eggs as described.

Or when you got good wood on the ball.

It's not been when you got good wood on the ball.

Nor been looking like you were coming close to getting any kind of wood on the ball when it was your mother and your father who were there for them to see you looking like it. No, not been when your mother and father were there when it would have looked to anybody like you were getting all set for you to get some good wood on the ball—or get any kind of quality of anything on anything and then of them seeing you look like you were doing it, or were going to do it, or did it, just did.

Because I said, because I am saying forget all that, forget all of these things like things like that. Such as please go ahead and forget things like me reading things or like me sitting in the chair I used to squunch all around in for me to sit in the chair and read things in it the best way anybody could sit in that chair and read things in it or sit in any other chair for me to sit and read a thing in it.

Or things like me fucking in a chair.

Forget things like me fucking in a chair.

Like me sitting fucking Helen in the chair which, you know, which, okay, which Helen had.

Like sitting fucking Helen in the chair with us the both of us sitting facing the mirror facing the chair that Helen, which Helen had.

Or even fucking Helen's sister like this.

With Helen facing Helen's sister and me and with me fucking Helen's sister like this.

Well, with the mirror facing all of us sitting and fucking and looking and facing the mirror like this.

And it was everything to me, everything.

But even if it was everything to me, was it the best thing of all of the everythings in my life to me?

Because it wasn't, it wasn't.

Or weren't you paying attention when I said none of these things were any of them anywhere close to them being the best thing in my life to me?

Because the best thing in my life to me—are you crazy, don't be crazy!—because the best thing in my life

to me wasn't any kind of a thing like any of these kinds
of a thing to me. Which goes, which also goes for the
day which was the first day of all of the brand-new
spring days for me.

I mean the one when it was okay for you to first go
out with your short pants on.

Not to mention short sleeves.

And in the air there was this smell in the air which
you could smell in the air which was like the smell of
smelling the sun in the air—or which, when you smelled
it, it was like smelling the beginning of everything
smellable in the air.

Oh, it was nice, so nice—the beginning of smelling
even the beginning of everybody dying in the air.

Am I not saying it was nice?

But the best?

My God, the best in my life to me?

Because the best in my life to me, it wasn't even coming with anyone.

Or getting off with anyone.

Or getting gone for good with any of the women.

Not even with Helen in the mirror with Helen's sister
in the mirror and with all of the women watching.

It was lint.

I'm sorry, but it was lint.

I'm telling you the answer is lint, it was lint.

You hear me?

Listen to me if you want to hear me—lint, it was lint—the best thing in my life to me, the most wonderful thing to me in my life to me, it was lint, it was getting the lint, it was getting down on my hands and knees with this hanger I went and got and getting down on my hands and knees with it and getting it opened up so it was all bent open and as unbent as you could get it to come out like it was this one long thing like a long wire thing and then sticking it down in under the dryer and sticking it all of the way back down in under the dryer and scooting it all of the way around and then scooting it all of the way back out to me again to me with all of these gobs of this thick gobby stuff stuck on it in like these big globs of this built-up lint on it.

So I tell you the thing.

But do you listen to the thing?

Because this was the thing which I am telling you which was the one best thing in my life to me.

Getting lint.

Getting all of that wadded-up lint.

Which came out in such globby gobs of it when I got down on my hands and knees with the idea of now is the time for me to go see what I can get out from down under way back in the back of under where it's underneath the dryer again.

Unless you think, unless everybody thinks hey, buddy, isn't the best is yet what has yet to come for you?

As far as referring, I mean.

I mean as far as me referring to what has been go-ing ahead and wadding itself up right back up again back down in under the back of in the back of there since.

As far as the dryer, I mean.

As far as the lint underneath the dryer, I mean.

Or wherever else the wadding never quits.

MERCANTILISM

THANK YOU FOR THE OPPORTUNITY to express my views and opinions. I am happy here. What is it. It is solicitous. Yet the dickens if I am not obliged to count another day when chicken a la king made no appearance for itself on the bill of fare. What can this mean. Is chicken fricassee also under fire. I have heard there are pressures. If forces are in sway, it is only fair I be told. Plus all thanks for my room. I used to be so crazy. I was really crazy. Throw your mind back to McCreery's. Maybe it wasn't spelled McCreery's. I used to have the impression a bug got in me from broccoli. Well, that's broccoli for you. I am a victim of constipation. It's my whole story. Is this really Bloomingdale's. I was in Russek's. I was in J. Thorpe. The biggest time I ever had was when I was in Wanamaker's and Arnold Constable's. Throw your mind back to DePinna's. Throw your mind back to B. Altman's. That's when there was smooth sailing with the chicken dishes. Remember chicken croquettes. So who is in the kitchen. Is there a procedure. Did I just worsen everything asking. What worsens things. I have to have more information. Which is it, laundromat or washateria. If I enjoy rights, I want to exercise them, thanks. They assigned me in Saks Fifth Avenue a sitting specialist as far as me sitting more conducively for evacuation purposes. I could use guidance. I would benefit from guidance. Well, here's hoping we see improvement. I'm no expert,

but this can't be democracy in action. What do you
think of this. Somebody such as myself sees their
mother and father hugging each other and shuddering
with each other when it rains on this pile of plywood
outside their window, or is it plasterboard. Please extend
to me the courtesy of answering. I'm looking for wide-
spread approval and pronominal agreement. You know
Korvette's, you know Filene's, you know Marshall Field.
There never was a dissatisfaction in the old era. I hate
to bother you with this. It's not I couldn't, if I put my
mind to it, live without chicken croquettes. It's curiosity.
Unless instead it's idle curiosity, which if it is, then fair
enough, no problem, I stand corrected. Rogers Peet,
Best's, they didn't want to come to grips with anything
in Rogers Peet or Best's. Oh my God, Abraham &
Straus and Peck & Peck and Gimbel's and Macy's. But
if the rule is no outbursts, then here's my word on it, I
never burst out. Praise be this is Bloomingdale's. Ever
see tots dragged around Abercrombie & Fitch. Mentally,
it's not sensible for consumers to say. Let's not split
hairs. I spoke without thinking. Long Island Lighting
Company and Brooklyn Union Gas. You ever hear of
Long Island Lighting Company and Brooklyn Union
Gas. What do you want to bet me, what do you want
to bet me they're Market Span now, that they're Market
Span now, and Sears Roebuck called me crazy. They
don't tell you on the transistor. They don't tell you on

the radio. Is this hypercritical. Please, did you ever come across anything as little as this is. The mistake I made dates back to Wallach's or Ohrbach's. In a word it was succotash. You can't wash anything too much. They speak of overwashing, but what don't they speak of. Look, if one thing is in there, then two things are in there. Work up your suds. Don't cut corners. Diligence pays off. Be thorough—plus that other word. Conscientious. I have not spoken concerning the Sunday Social Get-Together Hour. At the risk of monopolizing things, I would like to propose something. It's shy of an hour. It's short of an hour. Besides, I'm positive they're only oatmeal-flavored. There was a time when Bullock's was for everything this nation stood for. Don't take my word for it. I'm no whiz on elections. Another thing of vilification is what happened to the small fry. Please publish this with my name at the top of it, not at the bottom. Everything is so sick of being only itself. Well, you proffer your view and you proffer opinion and they sit there and take umbrage. It's a thankless job, don't worry, nobody's denying it. They're always so unappreciative of the pains you take. Well, they have their hands full. I was in Bergdorf Goodman when he was assigned to me. They act like you're mental. Facially, they were nothing to speak of. But at least the bill of fare, please, be serious, Swiss steak, Salisbury steak, pepper steak, you name it and it was accounted for, plus tapioca. This was America. Even in Klein's. Even in Two Guys. Even in May's or that other word, Walmart. They didn't stint. The kitchens blazed. This was back before the foreigners. This was when if you wanted light, if you wanted gas, then fine, fine, you opened your wallet and stated your wishes. They had things. They had desserts. It wasn't just all pleading innocent and mixing ammonia and bleach. If your mother and father don't tell you, who tells you. It's tragic what's going on. Is it down-to-earth. No, it is not down-to-earth. They tried stewed prunes on me. They knocked themselves out trying out stewed prunes on me. Morning, noon, and night, it was this constant incessantness of stewed prunes on me. The waste of it, the waste of it. How can everybody be fooled. They bamboozle you. The stewing industry gets together with themselves and pulls the wool over your eyes. You know the word hoodwink. You know the word bamboozle. Okay, so they pull a fast one—it's still pulling, it's still pulling, isn't it still the same difference. The dirty filthy rotten intelligentsia of it, Jesus. Wait a sec, wait a sec—hornswoggle, it's horn-swoggle. They talk about the jet stream, but do they mean it. Once a month you hear them saying okay, we're sending out invitations for another steak dinner in the White House, but is it cancer or what. It's not just here, it's not just there, it's everywhere. You know what we've lost—we've lost our frame of mind. And what about minute steak—show me one menu anywhere with a minute steak on it. Or pudding. What about butterscotch pudding. Sure, the chairs are comfortable, sure. Nobody said the seating was not accommodating and judicious. Did I imply otherwise. I did not hear myself imply otherwise. But on a personal basis, we can't just keep ignoring what's staring us in the face. It's ridiculous. I'm used to acrimony, I'm used to accusation, I'm used to recrimination, I'm used to invective. But no customer on earth should be required to take guff like this. I take umbrage. I am taking umbrage. People are human beings. You want to know what I'd like to know. I'd like to know just who exactly controls the controlling interest. But you make a stink and what do they do. It's atrocious. It's abominable. You know the cloche, I know the cloche, everybody knows the cloche, but does it make us one bit healthier. You go to the main floor. You begin with the main floor. This is what I am asking you. So then you say to yourself all right, fine, fine, I will venture up to the mezzanine. But does it matter to them. Do they honor you for it. Sometimes I just want to cry. Sometimes I just want to wave a wand and make everybody have to blow on their bisque in the same cafeteria. But there is not a one of them— not one, not one—which doesn't take the position they're a private dignitary. And another thing I would like to inquire of you—when it comes to views and opinions, where is the ileum. And what precisely does it have to do with Lord & Taylor. You wonder in your mind what's it all coming to, what's making it all keep going downhill like this, but when in the world was wondering its own reward. I lay it all at the feet of vindictiveness. To be absolutely frank with you, I couldn't look another fruit cup in the eye. But does this let anybody off the hook. This is no Penny's, this is no Bond's. This is Bloomingdale's, for pity's sake. Nevertheless, somebody gave the order for them to clamp down on the givens. Or is it distribution, distribution, distribution, distribution. All of a sudden you suddenly notice everything is persona non grata on the bill of fare. You know what happened to Robert Hall, don't you. Don't we have better things for us to do than for me to make a nuisance of myself. Yet who could warn prior administrations. The smartest people tried to reason with them, but would they listen. I'd sue if I wasn't just a figment of my imagination. I mean what I say—I'd get on the phone and get a lawyer and sue. I'd sue the broccoli manufacturers just on general principle. You think I'm being frivolent, but I'm not being frivolent. Things can also hide in string beans. If you were a thing in a pod, isn't it logical you would not be in sight in it. That's what happened to me even before I was aware of peas. Don't give me Bendel's, don't give me Burdine's, don't give me Bonwit Teller either. It starts with a vegetable. Or that other word, fruit. This is what it is to enact legislation. Watch for shifts. Be vigilant. Traditionally, when hasn't there been suspicion surrounding eggplant, kumquat, rutabaga, pear. First it flourishes, then it digs itself in, then it goes latent on you, or that other word, dormant. There is nothing that cannot come back to life as a nevus, as a clavus, as a papule, as a bleb. Don't expect me to make sense out of it for you. But neither should you brush me aside as a mere bagatelle. There is no action in political action. They want the wheel, let them have the wheel. You know the word joyride. You are familiar with the word joyride. Yes, I took the brunt of it but not because there was a ballot on it but because I know knavery when I see knavery. Plus underhandedness and mischief. This was the decade of the debate over due to and owing to, which one to cast your vote for, which one to cast your vote for, and now listen, now listen, will you just fucking please just listen. Because now it's all because, because, because, because. No one remembers, no one gives credit. Where are the mezzanines of yesteryear. You know what the battle cry once was. Give the citizenry gum. Bloomingdale's was the one hold-out. Is it still the one hold-out. This is what I'm asking. We believed in something. It's what our forefathers went to court for. It wasn't just Davega one day, Nordstrom's the next. There's not one speck of stomach for jurisprudence any-

more. Where's light, where's gas. You want to be smart.
Stay close to the radio. Get a transistor. Do you have
batteries. Stock up on batteries. I'm high. Get a high
room like I have. Mine could just sit and do it. Either
one of them, they could just say to you okay, I'm ready
to go and go. You're nuts if you think you can place any
confidence in pine or in the other word, maple. Trust
plywood. Even plasterboard if necessary. Remember
Johns Manville. Here's a bulletin for you. They cut in
and said it's Market Span. Forget Brooklyn, forget Long
Island—it's the dirty filthy rotten Bronx we better get a
committee together over and sit down and have an emer-
gency symposium for. You see what I'm saying about
passivity. It's alchemy. It's all this dreadful selfishness.
My advice is lend yourself to the reclamation of the
lowlands if you want anybody to believe you have any
sincerity as far as the struggle to develop wellsprings. It's
this thing in me. It's this old devil moon in me. Can
you just feature it, the two of them hugging and shuddering in the precipitation. Did I write to my congress-
man or to the contrary. I'm talking weatherwise, completely weatherwise. Free access to the window. Lax
groundskeeping. It's not like the old era when you had
your Montgomery Ward and that was that. It's simple
science. They come and swim up into you up inside of
you even if if if you never got down on your hands
and knees and had even one lousy irrigation. Or even

a nose drop. Look, are they trying to get us to subscribe to the idea chicken tetrazzini vanished of its own accord. Skip it. I am not retaining counsel. It was you and your thugs who sought me out, not to the contrary. Or that other word, shopping. Let alone inkling, how about inkling—so long as the whole thesis is only for everybody to sit around and act like they are better than I am and be just so fucking in a hurry about it.

THE PRACTICE OF EVERYDAY LIFE

WHAT IS IT? YOU THINK IT'S ME? If it's me, then, okay, then I'm not arguing, then it's me. But what I mean is am I just being too stippy-minded all of the time? Because some of the time I think I am all of the time being just too stippy-minded for my own good. Like take this word come which they use. How come it's come? Didn't you ever stop to think I don't get it how come it's come? How come people don't say go? You know, I'm going, I'm going, I'm going! I just for once in my life would like to hear somebody screaming my God, my God, I'm going! Oh, but they can't, can they? They say they're going and you think they're making a peepee. You say to somebody I'm going, the first thing they're going to think about you is what are you doing, are you making a peepee? Remember when your mother said to you will you please for godsakes go already? Remember when your mother would stand outside the door and say to you I don't have all day, so for godsakes will you please go already? My mother used to do that. My mother used to say make and go. Make was to, you know, make was for you to make a number two, whereas go, go meant do a number one. It was like make was like this productive thing, wasn't it? You make and, presto, if you did it, you made something. There was like this poiesis involved. It was like taking a dump was like having this poiesis which was involved. Okay, I am just thinking my thoughts out loud. Or how about this—how about aloud? You don't hear people saying aloud anymore. Who says aloud anymore? But so who's in charge of these things like this—humanity saying out loud instead of saying aloud? Remember when everybody used to call it a Coney Island Red Hot? There were these places that sold you these frankfurters and they called them Coney Island Red Hots. Forget it. You're not interested. I was just over at my friend Krupp's. I was just over at my friend Krupp's place, and I am trying to make this point to Krupp about something, I am sitting there trying to make this important point to Krupp about something, but all Krupp is doing is saying show Gordie how you can sneeze, Lulu, show him. Do I want to hear a dog sneeze? Is this like what the thing of my life has finally come to? I have to sit like a gentleman somewhere listening to a dog sneeze? I had a point to make. But does anybody want to hear the point you have to make? What they want for you to do is for them to get a dog to sneeze and make me have to be the audience for it. I used to be a serious person. I used to read things and have things to say about them. Now all I do is go around being an audience for everything, not excluding canines. There's this bum coming along wheeling along on the sidewalk with these five shopping carts rigged up like with these boards and things to make this one big crazy like overboard thing out of it with all of this wire and with a

radio going down in it somewhere and all this shit of his
in it and like outriggers. I spent days and days thinking to myself Gordon, what is the word for what that
looks like to me? Look, it's too complicated for you.
I'm not going into it with you because it's looks to me
like it's way too complicated for you. Like I see this
father in the park having a catch with his kid in the
park and the father keeps tossing the ball over the kid's
head and the kid keeps having to go hustling after the
ball and then has to keep coming all of the way back
with it to where he was so that when he throws the ball
the kid won't be too far away from the father for the
ball to get to the father when the kid tries to throw the
ball back. You know how long I stand there and watch
what I just told you? You would not believe how long
I stand there and watch it, this sad sorry sight like that
like just what I just told you. But like it's necessary for
me to do it is the sum and substance of my thinking.
I'm witnessing, I'm witnessing. It is an act of sociable
conscience as far as I go as far as, you know, as the grief
of the kid in this context goes. Who else is willing to
do this? Do I see anybody else who is willing to do
this? I'm in this video store asking for these great old
movies from the great old days and there's this kid there
with his mother there and I am listening and I am hearing and can anybody believe what I as an involved by-
stander am hearing? Because check me out on this—it's

the same little kid screaming no, I am not getting any fucking movie with any fucking sword-fighting in it, it's either people shooting or I'm telling! Actually, I have to tell you something, the kid's theory of thinking, you have to go along with it, shooting's better. But here is the other thing—who's he think he's telling, the father? I mean, it's the same father, right? But honestly, how come people stand there and say that, I'm telling? So who are they telling? Oh, excuse me, excuse me, whom— I'm fucking sorry, whom. So did I tell you about there's this lady I see pick up this mitten I see her see on the sidewalk and goes and sticks it up on top of this fire hydrant like it is going to be up there for it to say hello to all of the passing parade and asking them hey, hey, did any of you losers lose me? Go tell her. She is probably somebody who you can tell. Man oh man, I should have gone up over to her and told her about all of these things which I'm telling you about, exclusive of the thing about her herself. A concerned citizen. A responsible member of the socialist framework. I bet anything that lady is a serious individual just like I used to be. Boy, do I miss it, being the conscience of the people. Now all I do is go around stealing toilet paper from places and being everybody's public person so they can look at somebody and say him. Oh, schooner! It just came to me, schooner. Lucky thing for you I am the kind of a human being who keeps going after things even when they go way over my head. I'm sorry. That was uncalled for. I guess I just wanted to get in another go again by way of making this look like I am trying to make this look like I maybe really made something. And another thing—right, right, I should have said his. Which is the whole point of the thing, isn't it?

His?

Meaning mine?

Fine, then make it weewee, fine.

CRAW

YOU KNOW ABOUT HANDEDNESS? Jesus, don't make me have to explain it to you about handedness. For Christ's sake, it's supposed to be something everybody knows, this way for this, that way for that. It's the rule of the whole works, one thing on the one hand, the other thing on the other hand. Isn't something as dumb as even a teacup handed? I'm almost positive of it, I am absolutely almost positive of it, even though there is absolutely no reason why I should have to know a thing like this about a teacup, is there?—because, oh come on, why should I, why should I, haven't I always been the same side of the way I'm handed as far as a teacup? Haven't I all of my life always been the same side as far as that? Which is why I am so incredibly pissed off with myself. I'm serious. I never used an expression like that, I have never once in my life ever before used such an expression as that, and this just goes to show you how exactly pissed off I am. Because I really am. And it's at myself, or with myself. And it's on account of something so incredibly stupid which I did which I really can't believe I did. It's hours now, it's been hours now, it's been almost half the day now since when I did it, and I am not, if you don't mind, I am not one bit less pissed off with myself even now after all of these hours later—I'm not, I'm sorry, I'm not! I expected it to, you know, to go ahead and dissipate. I expected it to like recede on me or something. Or from me. I expected

I'd, you know, that I would get used to it. But forget it. It was a bitter pill then and it's a bitter pill now and I bet it is going to remain being a bitter pill stuck up inside of me in my craw until I kill myself. Because I'm sorry, but this is just how I feel—that the only solution for this is for me to kill myself. I mean, Jesus, how could I have been so stupid? I've got some nerve sitting here accusing a teacup when look at me. Who would believe this? Nobody would believe this. I am too ashamed even to tell you what I did—except for the fact I glued something and that when I glued it I paid no attention to the handedness of it—or anyhow the handedness of me. Okay, I dropped something, okay? I dropped this particular thing and, right, you bet, it broke all apart, okay? But so then I thought to myself hey, it's not so bad, it's not so terrible, cheer up, for Christ's sake, can't you glue? I mean I thought to myself dummie, you can glue it, dummie, don't you see you can glue it? So I go get out the glue. It's this great glue. It's this glue which they invented for when it's glued, that's it, that's how it is, it is really fucking glued. What I mean is is that with this glue if you try after that to get it apart after that, like the thing you're gluing after you glued it, you break it but really good. Because this is how tough this glue is. It's some kind of wonder glue, this glue, and this is what happens with it, this is what's the final deal with it, you get your one chance with this glue and that's it. So did I know this? I knew this. There was no question in my mind that I knew this. You can't say okay, the guy didn't know what the score as far as this glue was because I knew it, I knew it, I did, I did. Except I didn't make any allowance for this handedness thing, did I? I glued it for the wrong hand. It was supposed to go this way and I sat there and glued it for going that way. So now what? It's glued. It looks like it's new and it works like it's new, but it's glued for somebody who goes the other way than I go. And I keep sitting here thinking to myself there's got to be a way for me to get this thing cleared up. Because I cannot accept the fact I went ahead and wrecked everything in my life—I mean really absolutely went ahead and wrecked it as far as this gluing—for good.

Just because I didn't think.

Just because I did not stop and say to myself look, dummie, are you stopping and first taking every little thing into an intelligent account of everything first?

Of course, there's always the solution of I could turn myself around. I'm not kidding. Why couldn't I solve the whole thing by just developing in myself the knack of turning myself the other way around? Or is it your opinion I should just kill myself and throw it all away and go out and get a whole new different one? But isn't that interesting, isn't it? Because if it could be different, if it could be different, then why couldn't I be different, especially because of the fact I am a human being and what the fuck is it but just a fucking thing that's now all turned around?

Is it even a teacup?

It's not even a teacup!

Oh God, I am so upset. I really cannot begin to tell you, I am really pretty goddamn fucking upset. And listen to me, just listen to me—breaking with fucking tradition, going ahead and fucking breaking with my own whole tradition and actually saying pissed off to people.

You probably are thinking to yourself okay, he's just horsing around, all the guy is doing is just sitting there just horsing around with people, but I'm telling you, ending it all, just turning around and ending it all, maybe it's really for the first time the right idea.

Unless it's actually the left one.

LOUCHE WITH YOU

YOU GOT SOME TIME? Because there's some stuff I'm getting off my chest. That's how come I'm doing this. It's this stuff. Stuff starts getting accumulated and if you don't get it cleared out from time to time and get it off your chest, there could be trouble from the build-up in your mind, no telling what. It's like jism. You get too much of your jism backed up on you, your prostate goes haywire and so do your nuts, is what the latest medical theory just so happens to say. So it goes right down there on my calendar every fifteen weeks: beat off. In case I forget. Ah, forget it. I'm lying. I'm not being straight with you. I am being, you guessed it, louche with you. There isn't any stuff that's built up. It's just the opposite. Nothing is. Nothing's building up in me anymore. It's just all just this drift and loss thing, drift and loss. I lost this great scarf of mine yesterday. It was more of a muffler than a scarf, if you really want to know what it really was. Anyway, I lost it. Was drifting along looking for a new kitchen sink. The kitchen sink I've got is getting all dingy-looking on me to my way of thinking and so I go out looking for a new one and I didn't find anything because there wasn't anything in the size of my old one and they told me my old one is so old they don't even make anything in the same size of it anymore and so I either get a new kitchen counter to handle the new kitchen sink or I have to learn to adjust myself to the old dingy-looking kitchen sink, which is what I am prepared to do, which is what I could not in my mind be that minute more prepared to do, but does this mean I have to lose this great muffler of mine just to come to this new-found conclusion of mine? So I was saying—so nothing's building up—jism included. It's like everything's getting away from me all of a sudden. It's like even when I say all of a sudden I suddenly this instant think people aren't saying all of a sudden anymore, are they? You think this is age or is it me? Like there should be a comma in there is the way Miss McEvoy taught me how to do it but I am all of a sudden scared that if I go back and put the comma in, it will mean to people fuck, this guy is really a fucking aged-type guy. And now look, shouldn't there be another one before but? I'm afraid. I'm afraid if I keep on doing things the way I have always done things, it'll be, we'll say, let's call it that it'll be this X amount of drift and loss, but if I don't, if I go ahead and, you know, change my ways, then the amount of drift and loss will instead be this Y amount, and so okay, this is the problem, which amount is the worse amount? That's what I'm afraid of—X or Y. I mean, listen—I don't want to keep hanging on to what's outmoded anymore than anybody else does, but what's going to happen to me if I let go of the outmoded stuff and—okay, this is perfect, this is perfect!—and "get a whole new kitchen sink," allegorically-speaking? You know what worries me the most actually? Let me tell you what actually, now that I think about it, worries me the most. Okay, so I go ahead and I adjust my way of thinking and learn to live with the dingy-looking sink and then somebody comes in here of another generation and they look and they say to themselves Jesus Christ, this old guy's a pretty sad fucking case, now isn't he? I mean, didn't I do it in my time myself? Didn't I, when I went to where my mother and father were keeping themselves when they in their time got to be pretty sad fucking cases of agedness themselves, didn't I in my time look at their things and say to myself Jesus, how do these people, how do my own fucking mother and father, how can any-body ever let their X and their Y get into such a dingy-looking situation like this?

Like just, in their case, the toilet seat.

God, I am already getting sick from just seeing it with the eye in my mind. So, fine, so we won't speak of it. Better if we do not speak of it. I am not permitting us to proceed as promised and, you know, and speak of it. But you get what I am getting at, don't you? Whereas my own personal toilet seat, it's okay, I am keeping close tabs on it, I do not let it out of my sight for one instant, but the kitchen sink, but what about the kitchen sink? You think they can't come in and give your toilet seat a satisfactory rating but then right in the same breath one lousy look at your kitchen sink sends the dirty stinking rats mincing right back out the door again with their stinking vicious filthy tongues wagging? And could you run after them and call out to them wait a sec, hang on a sec, it's just this thing which just so happens to right now be going on with me as per my period of me adjusting?

It's no good.

People don't give you any credit for you adjusting.

This is the whole thing of it with people—they sneer at you behind your back even though all you are doing is you're just coming around to another period of you adjusting. I'm telling you, as far as people, all adjusting is maladjusting or else forget it.

But losing things like mufflers, this is where we have to draw the line. This muffler in particular. Because this was honestly some muffler I had. You couldn't go out and buy a muffler like this muffler no matter what generation the people are saying you're a member of. It was one of a kind, this muffler of mine. People used to stop me on the street and get up close to me and take a good sharp look at me and say to me, "Mister, this muffler you got, no kidding, it's definitely a honey."

But days like those days, hey, they're gone for good now, days like such as those days.

Never mind.

What's not gone for good except the nights?

And the awful algebra.

Nor need it be added—the nocturnal build-up of untold rue until—fuck!—I'm dead from it and didn't even go with a warm neck.

PHYSIS VERSUS NOMOS

SO I SAYS TO THE WINDOW-SHADE MAN, I says to him you see this window shade, this window shade's no good, this window shade is beat to shit, this window shade has been in my window since who knows when, I need a new window shade, how about a new window shade, you got another window shade for me just like this one, and so the window-shade man takes the window shade from me and the window-shade man, he says to me just like this one, just like this one, there can be no window shade just like this one, even this one cannot be just like this one when you said to me just like this one since this one is now not a window shade in your hands, this one is now a window shade in my hands, whereupon I says to the window-shade man yeah but barring all that, but barring all that, let's get down to cases, cases, says the window-shade man, you want cases, says the window-shade man, here's cases for you just to begin with, says the window-shade man, as in see this grommet you got here in this window shade, what we do here is we don't do a thing like this grommet you got here, you want a grommet, you don't come here, you want a grommet in it as far as a window shade, you go down the block you get a grommet in it as far as a window shade, down the block they do it for you with a grommet in it for you as far as a window shade for you, here we do it with you screw in this thing here like a button here and then the pull itself, you take the loop like this and it goes around and winds around it like it's like a button you're winding the loop of the pull around, but grommet forget about it, grommet you're spinning your wheels, you have to have a grommet in it, then we are not the window-shade people for you and your people, you have to have a grommet in it, the window-shade people for you, these are the window-shade people down the block or up the block depending on which direction, that's where they do a grommet, that's where you get a grommet, this place we don't do a grommet, this place you can't get a grommet, us what we do here is you get home and you screw in this screw-in thing which is like a button we give you at the bottom in the stick on this side, on that side, whichever side you want and then the pull, all you do is you take the loop and go wind it any way you want to wind, the wind is up to you the way you decide you want to wind it, but a grommet, not a grommet, you want a grommet, you go to the other people, they can do a grommet for you if a grommet is what you want, but so are we doing business with you or are we facing an impasse with you as far as the stipulation with the grommet with you, and so I says to the window-shade man, I says to him the only thing different if I go ahead and get the window shade with you people and not with the other people is with you people the grommet, it's just the grommet, or is what you're telling me is there are other things which

you are going to tell me which are also in the nature of
things which are going to be different as far as the window shade we're getting rid of, whereupon the man says
to me, whereupon the window-shade man says to me
brackets, let's talk brackets, let's review what at your residence the situation is as far as brackets, which way are
you set up in your residence as far as your brackets, and
so I says to the window-shade man brackets, you mean
when you say brackets you mean these like bracket
things which they go up there where you screw them
into the wall with like these anchors or something, plugs,
up into the insides up at the top of the window and you
get up and you hang the window shade from them, like
these two little things which one of them goes on one
side and the other one goes on the other side, those
things like brackets are what you mean when you say to
me brackets, and so the window-shade man says to me
sided, they're sided, they're like one side is for one side
and the other side is for the other side on the other side,
so the question which I am asking you is which way do
you want for us to set you up with the window shade
we're making for you as far as replacing the old window
shade with regard to the question of conforming to the
old brackets, or is it in your thinking at this stage of the
game what you want for your agenda to look like is you
take out the old ones which went with this window
shade here and get us to give you new ones so you can

start over fresh from the beginning with new ones, in which case don't forget we also have to charge you for new plugs as far as anchoring it, and so I says to the window-shade man, I say to him look, it should only all I know is roll up so it's rolling up on the outside and not up on the inside and so it's facing out on the side facing into the window, this cuff down here at the bottom where it turns around and makes the opening where the stick is, or goes through.

"Oh," he says.

"What's the matter?" I say.

The window-shade man says to me, "Go home and look it over and get your agenda straight before you come in here with things like this for me when you are obviously so obviously ill-prepared to go ahead and do business with me as your preferred window-shade tradesperson in the neighborhood." The window-shade man says to me, "This is not a criticism. Don't take this as a criticism. It is not my policy here to stand here and offer criticism." The window-shade man says to me, "I am giving guidance. I am giving counsel. Do not take it as a rebuff. Do not take it as a reproof. First go see what's your setup as far as the specifics is so you can come in here unencumbered and act freely like a human being unfettered by the conditions."

So I say to the window-shade man, "Look, believe me, I am here on your premises in good faith and am ready and able to do business with you with a clear conscience as a fully endowed citizen in complete possession of his wits as well as his teleology."

"Yeah," the window-shade man says to me, "but I'm not arguing, it's not an argument, no one here is standing here endeavoring to take issue with you as far as an argument, but the brackets," the window-shade man says to me, "your qualification with the brackets is they go this way or they go that way, which is not for one minute to say they can't go up and get screwed in either way which you want them to, but once they're in on whichever side which you screw each one of them in on, everything devolves from that fact and therefore develops the repercussion of which way the window shade rolls, does the window shade roll in or does the window shade roll out. So you understand what I'm saying?" the window-shade man says. "Devolves or debouches."

"How could I not understand what you're saying?" I says. "I understand what you're saying," I says. "But I'm just saying myself," I says.

"Stay with me with this," says the window-shade man. "You mention cuff. I heard you mention cuff. Okay, cuff. Talk to me, talk to me—you want the cuff you can see from the inside or you can't—which or which?"

"Right," I says, "right." I says to the window-shade man, I says to him, "This is the question," I says, "and the answer to the question is I don't know if I can answer this question with an uncluttered mind."

"Well, it's your brackets," the window-shade man says. "It all goes back to your brackets," the window-shade man says. "We're getting nowhere with this until we get a better grip on your past setup as far as brackets," the window-shade man says. "But," the window-shade man says, "this is where your age-old question as far as volition comes in. Plus, you know, plus ataraxy."

"You mean at home," I says.

"Check," the window-shade man says. "So what you do is you turn around and you go home and you get home and you look up there at the top of the window and you see what your situation shapes up like on a current basis as far as shall I say the sidedness of your brackets and then you turn around and you come back here to me here and you talk to me and the two of us will do business or not do business, but first we got to know what we are talking about as far as what is in the wall as of now and is it to continue on in it on the current basis or be reversed."

I says, "You want me to go home and look."

He says, "That's it—you go home and you look."

I says, "Right, right, but like what am I looking at?"

"Where you stand with the brackets," says the window-shade man. "What your setup is as far as the brackets," the window-shade man says. "What's what as far as the current sidedness when you get up on a stool and you inspect each respective bracket constituting the totality of your brackets non-dereistically."

"And that's it?"

"Providing we don't come to an aporia as far as the cuff and so forth," he says.

"But no grommet is what you're telling me no matter what, an affection for dereism notwithstanding."

"No matter what, you get no grommet for the pull, not here. What you get here for the pull is you get this screw-in thing we give you instead. See? Like a button. It's like a button with this like screw-in thing it's got on it sticking out going one way. Whereas what you already got yourself here on this one, it's a grommet. See this? This is a grommet. But me, when you do business here in this place with us as your window-shade people, it's exclusively this button treatment which I give you—lucid yes or lucid no?"

"Definitely, definitely," I says to him. "But so I should like go home, you're saying to me," I says to the window-shade man.

"Go home," the window-shade man says to me.

"See what the setup is."

"The situation," the window-shade man says to me.

"Check it out," I says.

"Check out the brackets," the window-shade man says to me. "Then you come back here and we get down to cases with a grasp of what the score is. Or you go up the block. Because you can always, you know, go up the block. There is always the freedom of you go up the block. Because with some people it's grommet and the question of the cuff is secondary or even absent."

"It's not a factor with me, I don't think."

"The grommet's not."

"The way I feel about it now at this stage of the game, the grommet is a non-issue."

"I know this," the window-shade man says. "I appreciate this," the window-shade man says. "I have every confidence," the window-shade man says.

"I can go with the screw-in," I says to him.

"The button," he says.

"I can definitely go with it," I say.

"Go home," says the window-shade man. "Get up on a stool. Take a look. See what your situation is. Look at it honestly. Take an honest look. Then if there is something for us to discuss as business people, I promise you, we will go ahead and discuss it."

"As people doing business," I say.

"Ah, yes, caught Homer at his nodding, did you? Yes, of course—as you say, as you say—as people doing business," says the window-shade man.

"In his nodding, I would say," I say.

"In? Yes, yes—in. Or caught out at, of course," the window-shade man says.

"So I go home?" says I to the window-shade man.

"That's it," says the window-shade man. "Unless it is your wish," says the window-shade man, "for us to linger over any of these imponderables of ours."

"Perhaps upon the occasion of my return," say I.

Says the window-shade man, "Should you choose for there to be one, that is. For there is the shop up or down the block," says the window-shade man.

Says I, "But it goes with me or stays here?"

Says the window-shade man, "You mean this window shade here. You mean while you go elsewhere, do you leave this window shade here."

"Home," says I. "Home only," says I. "Not elsewhere at all," says I.

"I don't know," says the window-shade man. "It is for you as a person of reflection to resolve," says the window-shade man. "There are difficulties I cannot resolve for you," says the window-shade man.

So I says to him, "But it's decidable, you think."

The window-shade man says to me, "I think—yes, I think. But now I think no—from your point of view, it's maybe too apophantic for you."

So I says to him, "Yet mustn't something be done one way or the other?"

"You're saying this to me as conjecture?" he says.

"Am I conjecturing?" I say.

"You want to determine if you are actually, in saying what you said, formulating a conjecture," he says.

"Absolutely," says I. "But at another level, you could lock the door."

"I could come to believe business hours had come to their end," says the window-shade man.

"Where's the law?" says I.

Says he, "Belief and the law, you're saying to me belief and the law, they cannot be tessellated?"

"Friendly relations, it makes for friends?" says I.

"Well," says the window-shade man, "extensity and intensity, there's always all that, isn't there?"

"Scum-sucking swine," says I. "Grommetless dog."

"Not grommetless, sir!" asserts the window-shade man. "Never been proved grommetless!" asserts the window-shade man.

"Point," says I. "Therefore," says I, "speak not to me of gussets," says I.

"But see you, don't you see you," says the window-shade man, calmer not by half but by much, "that are we not, in this matter, made claimants, then, the pair of us, on common but non-relational ground?"

"Good," says I to the window-shade man.

"Which makes this mine," says I to the window-shade man, leaving the window shade to keep to its place in the hands of the window-shade man and plucking the fascia from the face of the window-shade man, no more himself a window-shade man than I a shopper in want of even infrequent dark.

ANOTHER FELONIOUS DISCHARGE
OF SOVEREIGN PLENITUDE

AMONG THE POMERANIANS

THE GIRL IN LOVE LEANT her head away from him. The girl in love let her head come to rest against the head of the young woman sitting to the other side of herself. The man loved this. The man did not love the girl in love. What the man loved was that the girl in love was doing this thing she was doing and how the girl in love did it, letting her head lean ever so lightly to the side to let it come to rest against the side of the head of the young woman sitting to the other side of the girl in love—and sighing—oh, sighing—and turning one of the rings on her fingers and smiling into the amazed space in front of her and murmuring madly to the other young women—the girl in love's friends, the girl in love's so very, she said, cherished friends—madly murmuring to them of love—oh, love, love!

Were they to be married?

They were to be married.

Truly?

"Yes, of course—truly," the man said.

But when, when?

Soon—possibly soon—immediately upon their arrival in the great nation of America.

America?

Yes, America.

The United States?

Yes, yes, isn't it wonderful, the United States!

Oh, love, love.

But the man did not love the girl in love. The man loved no one, had loved no one, would love no one, though the man loved, would love, without limit, without reservation, irrevocably, indelibly, this gesture of the girl in love's, this occasion of the gesture's occurrence, of all the infinitely divisible occurrences swarming furiously upon the moment—the phosphorescence in the vast kitchen, the very word phosphorescence—to contrive to make the occurrence occur and to produce upon the man the effect of a thing for the man to love.

But not a person.

Never a person.

The girl in love leant her head away from the man. Something in a pot was heating on the stove. Was it coffee? Ah, no, it was not coffee. What, then, if not coffee? Oh, special, something special—wait and see, oh just you wait and see, you devil you.

Oh yes, to see, to see, to hear, to hear—the women madly murmuring, these wondrously wonderful women all murmuring madly into the amazed space of the vast kitchen—the girl in love with her head leant away from the man so that her head lay against the side of the head of the large woman who sat to the other side of the girl in love, if indeed the girl in love was a girl in love, or was even a girl.

The great éclair.

They had brought it with them—so festive, so very

festive—a pastry, the pastry—in celebration of this very festivity—a celebration of love—oh, love, love.

Dango-dango, a dango-dango.

It was called this, the pastry was actually called this—called, good God, a dango-dango—did you ever? But how grand, how so very grand—that such a way of speaking of a thing could possibly exist in a world where people had to speak of things—well, a dango-dango indeed and not just a giant éclair.

The girl in love leaned her head away from the man in order that the girl in love might bring her head to rest against the head of the large woman sitting to the other side of the girl in love, her eyes glistening, their eyes glistening, everyone's eyes glistening—the strange light making everything it fell upon—if the man cared to look at what the light fell upon, if only the man cared to get a good close look at it all—glisten.

Something was heating on the stove.

There was a pot of something heating on the stove.

The pot, the pot, wasn't it as well, didn't it too, wasn't it also glistening ever so strangely?—as if a radiance had been conceived in the very idea of its being a pot in which something was heating gently heating on a stove.

Well, a phosphor, then.

Chairs had been moved to the table. A bench had been brought up from a wall and positioned to one side of the table. This was where the girl in love sat with the

large-bodied friend whose head it was the girl in love
was resting her head against—on the bench drawn up to
the table and positioned to the one side of the table—
the man seated there at the table in the position, the
post, the post, of importance. There was music, wasn't
there?—voices, the voices of men, men's voices, as in a
solemn chanting from somewhere elsewhere, audible to
the man in this room but believed by him to issue from
some other room, the source, the man concluded, not
here but elsewhere, somewhere elsewhere. But where
elsewhere was there? How many rooms in all would
there be here, how many? Oh, there was so much the
man did not know—could not know, could not have
imagined it would have mattered for him to know,
would never, when it came to that, ever come come ever
to know. Well, the man was not exactly a dolt, was he?
I mean, he understood the one word meant wine, didn't
it?—because, after all, it was a bottle of wine, wasn't it?—
but the other word, what about this other word, what on
earth did this other word mean?—holy or health-giving,
sacred, sacrosanct, not unclean?

They sat at the table, those that were just now sitting.
And who were these who were just now sitting? Why,
the man, of course. The man was sitting. The girl in
love, she was sitting at the table. And to the girl in
love's other side, to the other side of the girl in love there was
sitting another girl, another young lady, another large-,

even larger-bodied, woman—the heads of the two very large women touching in such a manner as to tear at the man's heart, such as the man's heart was present in him to be torn at. And the foil, what about the foil, what had happened to the foil? Had the foil been torn? It was difficult for anyone to see, wasn't it? Or was seeing, was seeing anything, was really seeing any of these things, was it just a difficulty only for the man? The light in here—well, it was like a phosphor, wasn't it? The light was phosphorous, phosphorescent—a weak pulsing, a kind of throbbing pulsing, a pulsation that was deeply luminescent.

Ah, luminescent, luminescent.

The man understood he would one day tell of all this eventfulness, tell of the details constituting the eventfulness, grouping them together for the entertainment of all comers, and if no one came, if no one in the world ever came to hear the man say luminescent, then no matter, no matter, then the man would group together what he would group together only for himself, so that, yes, of course, of course—this long-ago eventfulness would prove to be an entertainment if only for himself—luminescent, a luminescence—I tell you, these words, the very abundance of them, how superb. Dim? No, not dim, never dim, but phosphorescent perhaps, luminescent perhaps—like a glimmering, yes, a glimmering. The light, it was like a glimmering, wasn't it? The light—ah, it fairly glinted, didn't it? It made things glint. It gave things to glint. So that things—glinted. So that everything—well, it glinted. So that there was this bounty of glintings in this domestic vastness—so that in the very vastation of the amazed space there was a definite, well, an indefinite distribution of hazy glintings—the pot, the forks and spoons, the spoons and forks, the bottle of wine, the wine bottle, the water tumblers for the wine, the knife, the immense the ridiculous the ridiculously too severe—but quaint, yes, quaint—kitchen knife. For example, for further example, the patina of the table, for even further example—another glinting, such a glinting—the man would say the table, that the table had been a patinated table, this, uh, well, this refectory table, it had shone, by Jupiter, had it not?—with a glinting— the lovely young ladies having seated him at it in such a manner as to situate the man in the one important position at the table—honoring the man, yes, for was not the man being honored?—while the two of them, while two of the large women, while these were the large women who were the ones who were sitting side by side on the side of the table where the bench had been placed, the bench having been drawn up to the table from the wall where the bench was kept, the heads of the large women touching ever so, well, so touchingly— while wasn't there yet another woman, a third woman?—while this largest-bodied woman of the three large-bodied women, while this other one, that one, while she bustled all about in the amazed space, fussing all about with this sort of magisterially fussy bustling largest-bodied womanly air of hers—ah, seeing to things—seeing to the wine and to the water tumblers the wine would be poured into, seeing to the pastry and to the queer knife that would cut the pastry, that would slice the pastry, that would be stuck point-first down into the heart of the pastry to divide the wounded pastry into certain unimprovable portions of pastry, seeing to the forks and to the dishes and to the spoons and to the marvelously crude napkins and to the heavy Tuscan cups, was it, or to the heavy Norman cups, was it, that had been distributed to various sites on the table to accept into them whatever it was, the man decided, that was heating gently gently heating on the stove.

No, vastation didn't mean that. What in the world did vastation mean? And why three of them, these mugs, these cups, why only three of them, when weren't there four people present? Oh, so many present—so many.

These superbly heavy Bavarian mugs.

Or cups, were they? Were they instead to be called not mugs but cups?

Ah, yes, but wouldn't the man have some of it?

"But of course he will have some of it! My precious will have all he desires of it!" the girl in love answered for the man in the wonderful way these wonderful people had, confections all of them, weren't they?

Ah, the man—a delicate fellow, a fellow nowhere near the size of these oversized women and, since delicate, a man not unrespectful of things—a careful man, an aware man, a fellow not uninformed, for example, in a not very reliable way, of what style of table a refectory table would in fact be and rightly guessing that this wretched thing the three of them were sitting at, that it was no refectory table at all, not at all, but that it was just an ordinary sort of kitcheny thing made of some kind of ordinary kitcheny material meant to furnish durable service for the hard business kitchen work sometimes, in certain extreme cases—call them solemn, call them solemn—called for—but the word, the word refectory, refectory, would it not go far toward abetting the impression the man would want his tale to get across to all when all would want to hear of this mad murmuring romance of the man's when this mad murmuring romance of the man's had come at last to its mad murmuring annihilation and the man would stand restored to the country of his beginnings and to those to whom the man would then seek to address himself in order that the products of his travel might be enjoyed by all the stay-at-homes back home, those who would never themselves hear the mad murmurings in the earth?

How young was she, did you say?

Very young, would say the man—a shimmering young

bit of a thing, the man would say—and oh how it was, how wonderful it was that the very one kept letting her head come to rest against the head of the friend who sat next to her on the bench, oh my, my—and the ring on her finger, one of the rings on her fingers, that she was turning and twisting the ring, kept turning and twisting it, and sighing—oh, how the girl in love let herself sigh—into the amazed amazing conflagration underway?

Crepuscular, what exactly does it mean, crepuscular?

"Ah," the man would say, "the young ladies of the house, they sat us, this shimmering slip of a thing and me, they sat us down in some sort of marvelous sitting room, don't you know. At a refectory table—if can you feature it. Can you feature it?—this great this massive this humble walnut affair—or couldn't it have been made of some obscure but no less humble fruit wood?—so lightly patinated it was—or darkly, darkly—and the light, I forgot the light—the light in this kitchen of theirs, it was positively crepuscular. Or in the, you know, in the whatever it was of theirs. The refectory?"

Ah, the table.

It shone, it gleamed—didn't it really?

Formica.

A layered pattern—overlapping half-moons.

Iridescent.

Fruit wood—what does it mean, fruit wood?

Why would a wood be a fruit wood?

Was there not a platter being just now just now being reached down from somewhere just too high up in
the clerestory of this place for the man to exert himself
to look? But just see it now, now see it—the mad
pastry in its shimmering wrapping having been lifted
from where it waited in its paper and daintily ever so
daintily lowered upon it, the platter, this platter. How
was it that in this strange land that a mere serving dish
should come created in the character of what is this,
what is this?—is it not suggestive of the speckled egg-
shell derived from a, well, from a speckled bird? But
what of the wondrously silvery point of all attention, the
bright thing, that brightest thing, brighter than even the
brilliantly gleaming knife blade was bright—wasn't it
then that the very largest of the three so very large
women made her quick way to it and with such clev-
erly large long fingers, didn't the woman—oh, the girl,
the girl, then!—didn't she first undo the glittery tape the
bake shop had been applying to make a fancy package
of the treat as the man was pushing his hand down into
his pocket for him to extract from it the great lump of
money through which the girl in love would have to
sort for the man for him to present to the clerk the
strange bank notes that appeared to satisfy the matter?

But indolent—hmm, yes, he would say indolent.

But would he say confectionery?

Instead of bake shop?

"The air of the place, the kitchen, if it were a kitchen, it was redolent with indolence"—or would this be going too far for such a man, do you think?—"and there was this marvelous chanting effect that seemed to be encouraging this kind of marvelous under-effect of everything welling up from somewhere elsewhere. Voices of like men, I think—like probably like of monks, like of votaries, like of the, well, like of the ardent—cantorially speaking."

But, by thunder, in a world of dango-dangos, by Jove, how can there be any going any too far in anything in a world where confections came at you anointed with a moniker like that? For pity's sake, dango-dango, a dango-dango—did you ever in all your days?

Oh, love, love!—the man loved it, anointed with a moniker. Words, words—anointed, moniker, ah.

A thing you got in a bakery anointed with—or anointed by?—well, a moniker—going by a moniker—keep it plain, keep it simple, and watch it with the little words, oh the pesky these pesky these tiny little pesteriferous little words everywhere. But, anyway, no really, anyway, this too, this too, everything—it all, it all—it all of it so very fittingly fit the scheme of the narrative the man was assembling for when it all—better told than this, you may be certain—could be told.

Oh, he saw it, he saw it—the foil being collected into itself, the massive woman collecting the foil into itself for her to make a very correct bolus of the thing before discarding it—no, not discarding—say instead letting gracefully ever so gracefully go of it—so that the thing seemed to the man to drift luminously down into the dark hollow beneath the sink. Was there a receptacle under there? Oh, there had to be a receptacle down under there. Didn't there have to be a receptacle down under in there? But what man could be convinced of much in this crepuscular light? Yet the man could be certain of the teeth of the girl in love, for example—ah, her teeth, such teeth. The girl in love was smiling into the amazing space. Her ring, one of her rings, this one ring among her many many rings, she turned it, kept turning and twisting it, kept sighing and smiling, the large head leaning, leant up against the even larger head of the woman—oh no, of the girl, of course of the girl, the even larger head of the even larger girl who sat on the bench beside her—no, to the other side—who sat to the far side of the girl in love.

The man marveled—the man was marveling over everything—or marveling at it. At how the bustling about was like a languor—or was it that the languorousness of the biggest of the girls was somehow like a slumbrous bustling about everywhere actually—very managerial, magisterial, big-bodied, indolent—yet quick and exacting—or fastidious, this was the word, fastidious—massively fastidious even, really pretty massively.

Oh, everything was opposites!

Everything here was in such a state of being opposites here. Yes, wasn't this the only way to say it, that all here was so marvelously, well, just a jumble of opposites here?

Jostling opposites.

All these opposites jostling one another.

Or is it oppositions, oppositions?—and is it not each other, not one another but each other?

Well, everything was a jumble, wasn't it?—a murmuring madness—amazed and amazing—the large handsome little-toothed young woman—a girl, a mere girl—so wondrously in love with, of all things, the man, this man.

With such speed.

With such ease.

Or ease first and next, then next, speed.

Well, so much for travel.

It was wonderful to travel.

It was marvelous to travel.

The man had traveled, was traveling—had come to this land to get a bit of a travel in him taken care of. Wasn't travel experience?

Experience.

An experience.

And this was what it was to really have it, wasn't it?

The girl?

A girl in love insisting that she is what the story says she is—a girl in love—and in love—crazily, crazily—with this wonderful wonderful marvelous marvelous, can you believe it, American!

The girl in love sighed.

Her little teeth showed in her big sighing face.

There was something on the stove, heating. There was a pot of something heating gently gently heating on the stove. He would have some, wouldn't he? Your lover, your fiancé, your American from the United States, he would have some of this, wouldn't he? And the wine? Aren't we ready for the wine? Who is ready for the wine? But first—the dango-dango!

The man caught sight of the shimmering glimmering foil—the amazing paper. Someone was collecting it into a ball of some kind—a bolus, a bolus—and was now laying it—this was the biggest girl, the really biggest one, right?—was just now laying it ever so gracefully down into the dark well beneath the humble sink.

Oh my God, the sink.

The stone sink.

A sink made out of stone.

Humble, wasn't it?

And how had they got to this place? Wasn't it up, had the girl not led them up a long dark twisting turning oh so, well, so humble hill?

"My friends!" she had said. "My very best in all the world so lovely lovely friends!" the girl had said.

So-and-so and so-and-so.

Their names were so-and-so and so-and-so.

Well, it was hard for the man to hear.

He could hear voices, hear the voices of men—of the worshipful, the man imagined—chanting, or groaning, in a neighboring room.

He said, "Are there people here? It sounds like zealots or something."

Everything was so—well, glittery.

The light was downright crepuscular in here.

"The heavy Turkish cups—Morrocan—sacred, I think they were. Probably semi-sacred, don't you think? Mugs, ceremonial mugs, perhaps they were."

That's it!—it was tea, wasn't it?

A kind of tea was brewing, wasn't it?

Look at her, troubling herself to separate out the glossy tape the bakery had used to bind the glorious foil. The man saw somebody save the tape, wind it into a tight spool, then set the result to the side of something—of the humble sink, that humble cavity—so shallow, so very shallow, it seemed to the man from where he sat—a scooped-out effect in a stone that must have been cut from the very oldest of old stones. Wait a minute—didn't the spool just sort of loosen itself when the girl let go of it? Then what was the point of that, what was the point of it?—of tightening the tape like that into such a precise spool of it like that if it was only to lose its form, the tension spilling out of it—spooling out of it in an instant—when the thing had been set to the side of what was it?

Yes, the sink made out of stone—yes, to the side of the humble sink created from a humble stone.

Humble, everything so humble.

Well, the light in this place, whatever it was, it was so very crepuscular—by jiminy, this light in this place, isn't it altogether too terrifically crepuscular?

Her dress, one of them, the dress of one of them—its loose sleeves seemed to the man cuffed or turned up in some interesting way, or twisted oddly, oddly twisted— that was it, twisted—so that the immense girl's immense arms appeared to the man to be too visible, to be sort of angrily visible, great bulky things, great swollen things, angrily jostling the amazed air. But thank goodness the man could see that the dress she wore—who was this, which one of them was this, was it the one in love?— that it was a sort of cream-colored affair, wasn't it, the color of this dress.

The color of cream?

It seemed to the man that there was somebody whose dress was colored a sort of creamy color—that there was a dotted effect scattered all about—some sort of dotted device—or not dot, not dot, but pinwheels perhaps, per- haps pinwheels. Yes, there seemed to the man to be a sort of dotted pinwheely effect, brought forth into the light by a range of strengths—in maroon, in the color maroon. Well, mightn't washings, mightn't long sad riverbank washings account for the variation from here to there in the vividness, or lack of it, the lack of it, mightn't it be the variability in this, in long sad desert-bound washings—they beat cloth, didn't they?—whipping at it with long thin sticks—with reeds probably, probably with reeds—mightn't it be the hard washings—actually whippings—the cloth had undergone to get it clean that accounted for the weak effect of one pinwheel and then of another pinwheel and then of yet a further even weaker pinwheel—maroon, hardly even still maroon, so beaten into proud cleanliness this least of all the pinwheels was?

I mean, it wasn't a design, was it?

Some intentionality in it of some sort?

By design?

And where was the knife point?

The dango-dango, had they cut into it yet?

The man rather liked the notion of this rough homespun subjected to a furor of care unique to this large mysterious person, common to these large mysterious persons. The word chestnut occurred to the man. The word maroon. Weak maroon, a weakened maroon, whipped to only barely scarcely even hints of a maroon—just barely visible tiny tiny—well, pinwheels of a kind of tiny-hearted maroon.

Whatever pinwheels were.

And maroon.

How-hearted maroon, what-hearted?

It was cold in here, or cool, wasn't it?

"Oh, how lovely all this is—how lovely," the man murmured into the madly amazed space.

Hadn't he meant to say chilly?

Well, the man was certain someone was waiting for him to speak. So the man spoke. He said, "It's so terribly lovely in here." He said, "I am the happiest man there is in here."

Ah, perfect.

Splendid.

The man let himself settle back into the one good chair. He listened to the heating of whatever it was—tea—yes, it was tea—that was heating on the stove. The adorations of the adoring, their obeisances, superb, superb. Had the man ever heard anything more superb? Belief was a wonderful thing—marvelous, really—faith. Was there a sanctuary nearby? Was such a sanctuary actually here within? Were they in it? Is this what this was?—no kitchen, after all—not a scullery but a site where life leant over to huddle into itself in great grand occurrences of prayer?

"Perfect—perfectly perfect," the man murmured as he settled back into the vast depths—the vastation, isn't it permissible to say vastation?—of this very decent—an important piece actually—of this very good, though humble, probably emphatically sturdy humble chair.

The young ladies seemed to be looking at the man in very deep approval of this.

Or at—at this.

"Perfect," the man said, a little madly, he now thought. "Oh, this is perfect," the man said.

Yes, yes, a toast, somebody called—time for a toast! Mustn't something be said in testimony of this great happiness? But how conduct a toast when the cork had yet to be taken from the bottle? No wine had been poured yet, had it? Oh, these people, these perfect people, water tumblers in lieu of wineglasses and a wine that was devised as sacred and health-giving.

Or holy and so on.

As in consecrated and so on.

In lieu of, the man loved that, in lieu of. Oh such innocents, these big-bodied hill-dwelling people, such perfect—the lot of them—such perfect naifs—water tumblers in lieu of, of all the things in the world.

Instead of?

In place of?

No, in lieu of, in lieu of!

Sacrality, now there was a word!

Ah, well, what else did the man love?—apart, of course, from his loving in lieu of and loving how the girl was still keeping her head leant against the head of the girl sitting next to her, now the both of them sigh-

ing now, now the both of them sighing now into the
burning phosphor now, and smiling with little dots of
little teeth. Let me see, then, let me see—what else did
the man love, you ask me, what else?—well, you shall
have your answer, shan't you!—for this man loved, had
loved, would always love the tapping of his mother's fingernails tapping on the backs of playing cards. That, that,
and the way the woman had of shooting a look heavenward in hopeless appeal and of rolling her eyes at him,
one of the wives the man had had, or was it really indeed the man's mother who had done this?

Oh, that's a good one—those hads—a mad murmuring distribution of hads we of us who are still striving
to keep paying attention just had. Ah, but what a confusion of things this is getting to be—the man standing
amid such a confusion of things—or sitting amid it, settling deeply into the humble chair, the young ladies, no
more now than mere biggish impressions of amazingly
biggish things, forever seeming to him to be directing at
him looks of deeply satisfied approval.

Well, the wife was dead and the mother was dead and
people were only their repertoire of gestures anyway and
here was the man traveling as travelers will travel and
here all of a sudden was suddenly this mere biggish impression of a biggish girl now somehow traveling with
the man—and now look, will you please just look, all
these festive others now settling with the man into the

glimmering deep light of the crepuscular—as if the world had been lifted off its course and laid down into, laid ever so gracefully down into—no, let go of—gently gently falling falling—into a very, well, harem—say harem, then.

Or that other word.

Seraglio.

Say seraglio.

Ah, that was the one, that was the very one—at least as words go, it was—into a very, say, seraglio.

What a word, what a word!

At least as words go, what a tooter.

"A toast!" the man bleated.

Gad, but who says the man bleated?

Well, the man would not tell of this, of bleating. There would be no telling of this bleating, by gum. Had the man bleated? Had he, well, burped, belched, eructated? What on earth had the man done if not offered a toast? For the man had the sense—or, rather to say, impression, wasn't this the word, had an impression?—for there was this impression forming around him somewhere elsewhere, wasn't there?—perhaps in the man, perhaps somewhere to either side of the man, or all around the man—it was the impression of a kind of bleating or something eructating from somewhere elsewhere. Well, the man could have burped, could he not have? Or belched—or, you know, or eructated? The man could have eructated in a—of course, of course—eructated in a ructation, couldn't he have? Well, the wine—after all, the wine. And the man had done a fine job of it, hadn't he?—of getting the cork from the wine.

Or bottle.

Well, the man did not remember any of it—the struggle to get any cork out of anything, or which of them it was who had called out into the bleating air "Praise be the day!" What the man remembered was this—something was heating on the stove, something in a pot was heating on the stove, there was something in a pot that was heating heating gently gently heating heating on the stove.

The man spoke with enormous care.

"I feel sacred," the man said. "I feel healthy," the man said. "I feel," the man said, "as if I have been given health," the man said—"and a certain holiness. Or sacrality!—I mean sacrality, don't I?"

Was he bleating?

The man burped a little, or belched a little, and touched the tip of his finger to the lips of the girl in love, whereupon the girl in love took the tip of the man's fingertip between her little teeth and gave to it a little tugging nip to it with her little tiny teeth.

"Next time your nose," the girl in love said.

"Watch out it's not next time your nose," the man heard the girl in love say.

"What did you say?" the man said, grinning madly into the amazing eventfulness of this experience.

"Bite it, bite it!" either or both or neither of the other girls shrieked. But this was impossible. Everything was impossible. It was all these opposites ceaselessly disposed to opposing each other, or one another—in a state of ceaseless—well, of opposition, if you like. Ah, the devil take it, love!—yet when in all his days had the man ever seen anything anything anything lovelier?—this gesture of the girl's. The head-leaning. The head-resting. Combined with the murmuring, combined with the mad murmuring combinatory madness of it all—the smiling and the sighing and the sighing and the smiling. Well, hadn't her head—the head of the girl in love— hadn't it been laid to rest, or lain, lain, is it?—against the head of a nearby girl? Look, the main thing is this enormous cup. An altogether wrong sort of a cup for people to be drinking tea out of, isn't it?

Or mug.

Mexican, it looks like, doesn't it?

Tribal.

Humble.

Rudimentary.

Crude.

"Will you just listen to me!" the man said. "My goodness!" the man said. "Oh my goodness," he said.

How strange, the man thought, that a passion could

come about in any language, let alone in his own.

"Oh, but we are listening to you," said the one with the bright-bladed knife.

The stove—it was the tiniest humblest affair. It might have been a thing for a child to play with, though fire, although fire, burbled up from its one encrusted burner, a subtle, an even demure, flame.

Pinwheel.

What is a pinwheel, anyway?

Good heavens, is it possible for a story to be told when what is in it are only words?

There was a platter being reached down from somewhere very high up in this place. Wasn't one of the girls reaching down a platter from very high up above the head of the man up in the amazed air of the world far up above the head of the man somewhere altogether too terribly overhead in this place? Because wherever it was—given the man's age, given the man's ridiculous age—the event was altogether too high up for the man to be able to lean back his head far enough for him to give anything that high above his head a look to see what the event up over himself unbearably was.

Clerestory.

Hadn't the word clerestory once been sort of a part of all of this?

Oh, love, love!—here was the cake.

Behold the cake.

The great éclair, the celestial éclair.

The dango-dango, by God—it lay relieved of the foil and the foil lay dropped into the black well beneath the stone where—unseen, unseen!—the foil struggled to relieve itself of the folds that had been folded into it, strained to throw off the cruel twistings the cruel turnings all the multifarious cruelties folded into it to force its silver wing into the crusted lump of goo.

His money!

Where was his money?

Ah, my money, the man said to himself.

"Ah, my money," the man said aloud, touching the pocket where the great lump of money in it was still making a great comforting lump of itself all thick and becrusted on the man's chest.

The voices seemed ever so ardent, so urgent, these voices raised in oblation in a nearby place of prayer, or in prayer in a nearby place of oblation. Well, it's probably in or very near a kind of sanctuary of some kind. Perhaps some sort of hilltop, or hillside, or hill-bound—that's it, hill-bound!—retreat of some kind.

Redoubt?

A redoubt?

Well, where was this place, anyway?

Was this some crazy like claustral place like outside of somewhere elsewhere like some improbable land such as Turkistan or something?

Some abbey in Nepal, do they call it?

Or Tibet—perhaps in Tibet, in perhaps Tibet?

Oh, love, love!—the things we people will do and do again until done for for love.

His head hurt. His back hurt. His legs, they were finished. You'd had to twist and turn so many times for you to make it up the hill. The man had had to twist and turn so many times for him to make it up the hill.

It was oh so cruel.

So grotesque.

"To the happy couple!" the girl with the knife called out into the burning air.

Yes, yes, to the happy couple—of course, to the happy couple, yes of course—but this was so strange, such an expression as this in such a place as this.

The air burned.

Was burnt.

Was a phosphor scorched—had become a phosphorescence scorched to the very core of the word.

There was something heating. A pot of something, something in a pot—wasn't an ember of it still heating gently gently heating on the stove?

"To us!" the man bleated.

"By Jove, to all of us!" the man bleated, the ponderous cup—no, mug, call it a mug—leaden in his hand.

With all his might the man sought to elevate the massive vessel from the table, his uncontainable heart smouldering with the violence of choice.

Iberian.

Moravian.

Anatolian.

Sudanese.

Ah, it was somewhere along the Levant, of course.

"I had been having for myself a bit of a travel, you understand, and been putting up somewhere elsewhere, I do believe—along the Levant, was it not?"

Pomeranian!

Perfect, perfect—the stupendous cup, it was a Pomeranian cup—or Pomeranian mug. So that these, therefore, these females, didn't every large-bodied one of them have to be a Pomeranian female?

Oh, love, love!

The man had never been happier.

"Everybody, everybody!—I want you to hear this! I have never been happier, I have never been happier!"

Was this bleating?

Then so be it, if indeed it be it—a ructation, an eructation, of the bleating kind.

The man cared not. The man was happy. The man was a happy man—just able to twist and turn his head to see the girl in love with her head leant ever so cruelly just so. Leant, burnt, becrusted—wonderful, it was all so wonderful. Well, it put the man in mind of the word indolence. Yes, this was your authentic indolence for you, wasn't it? By golly, what I would like to know is this—is the smoking air redolent enough with enough authentic indolence for you? Oh, it all reminded the man of the way his mother had had of tapping her lacquered fingernails against the backs of playing cards—how the man had loved that, how the man had really loved that—and loved too the way the woman had of rolling her eyes at him in a show of what he took to be a sort of mock surprise at him—or bewilderment—or, that's it, in a sort of a show of a kind of a good-natured mocking befuddlement over him, of her regarding the man with a certain air of what you might have said appeared to be a kind of a genuine mock befuddlement with him, or over him, genuinely.

Unless it had been a wife of his.

Unless it had been one of the man's wives who had rolled her eyes at him. Who had lifted her eyes heavenward in a show of authentically mock consternation with him. But good-naturedly, good-naturedly.

Or at him.

Well, what matter which and who and all of that? It was only this that counted. But what, in fact, was this, anyway? And where was it, where?

Was he under the card table?

Was the man down under the table where his mother had played card games at the table, clicking her painted fingernails against the backs of the playing cards that the women, all the women, played with at the table?

No, no, of course not.

Hadn't the man made his way up some dreadful hill? Well, he had, hadn't he? And how on earth had he managed it, such a ceaseless twisting turning in the desperately angry heat, the immense child clunking along at his side as the man struggled to keep the grotesque pastry from leaning all the way away from him and with the torporous abandon of the inanimate sagging all the way away from him and slumping into the mad wild buzzing fields of Pomerania.

The girl had her head leant well away from the man.

Something in a pot was gently heating heating gently on the stove. They sat at the table, those who were sitting. The man understood he must tell of all this when he had been restored to his own country, and that, when he told, he would say the table had been a refectory table and that the devout could be heard in testimony of their devotions from the world next door and that somewhere elsewhere too far away for anyone to summon the strength for him to see it there was an ember glowing, there was an ember smouldering, as Pomeranian after Pomeranian prepared to sever into parts the gooey domain of the great éclair.

Why did the word chestnut keep occurring to the man? And vastation, not vastitude?

It was cold, or cool, for the season.

But didn't this all depend upon where it was the season was seasoning? Oh, seasoning, seasoning—the man rather liked such effects, and understood them to constitute the profit of his touring among the humble of the earth. Then there was the girl, the gigantic sighing child, and her even larger no less innocent friends—colleagues, the tiny-toothed thing had called them, and yes, yes, so they were and would be, colleagues, the lot of them, colleagues all in all of this amazing romance.

The man caught sight of the flame.

Or was it where the light caught the knife?

Let me correct that.

Meant where knife knife caught light light.

"To iridescence!" the man shrieked—or did I somewhere elsewhere, wherever I was, use this word already?—and looked about himself at the notice such aptitude seemed to provoke in his colleagues.

No, tenderness.

This was the one word—this one, this!

Tendresse.

Yes, they would do it, wouldn't they?—these colleagues all about him. No, confederates—may we not say, as the man himself must come to say, confederates? Oh, but of course confederates, and would they not in due course do it with nothing less than with—yes, yes!—than with the customary—nay, celebrated—expression of Pomeranian tendresse?

THE TEST

TOMMY IS HERE. HELLO, TOMMY. Does Tommy want to play? Where is Timmy? Is Timmy in the yard? Yes, there's Timmy. Timmy is in the yard. Is Bobby here? Is Andy here? What about Lew? Where is Lew? The other boys, they are not here yet. Bobby and Andy and Lew, those boys are not here yet. But Tommy is. Hello, Timmy. Hello, Tommy. Did Tommy come to play? Yes, Tommy came to play. Okay, Tommy, ask Mother for something for you to play with. Ma'am, may I have something for me to play with? Yes, Tommy, here is what Timmy has. Oh yes, I want what Timmy has. Do you know what this is? This is a spork, Tommy. What is a spork? Who can say what a spork is? I can, I can. A spork is half a spoon and half a fork. Do you know what this spork is made out of? Who can say what this spork is made out of? This spork is made out of plastic. Can you say plastic? Say plastic. A spork is half a spoon and half a fork and this spork is made out of plastic. My mother doesn't call it that. My mother calls that a foon. What did you say, Tommy? Did Tommy say his mother calls a spork a foon? Why on earth does Tommy's mother call a spork a foon, Tommy? I don't know, missus, I don't know. Very well, boys—play nicely while I start the sandwiches cut in quarters with the crusts cut off and make the chocolate milk. Oh, look— here is another boy, here is Bobby. Hello, Bobby. Here is a spork for you too, Bobby. Go and play with Timmy and Tommy, Bobby. Are Timmy and Tommy in the yard? Yes, Bobby, Timmy and Tommy are in the yard. See the thing Timmy started killing before Tommy got here? Timmy knocked it off a leaf. Timmy used his spork to knock the thing off the leaf the thing was creeping, creeping, creeping on. Timmy has a nail he went and got from the garage. But Timmy used the spork Mother gave for the job of knocking the thing off the leaf before Tommy got here. Can you remember the job? What was the job? The job was knocking the thing off the leaf the thing was creeping, creeping, creeping on. Can you say creeping, creeping, creeping on? Try saying creeping, creeping, creeping on. Raise your hand if you can say creeping, creeping, creeping on. Oh, look what happened when Timmy knocked the thing off the leaf it was creeping, creeping, creeping on. It's in the dirt, it's in the dirt! Is the thing creeping down in the dirt? Oh, look at the thing creeping down in the dirt. Where oh where could the thing think it is creeping down in the dirt to? Do you know where the thing thinks it is creeping down in the dirt to? Look, everybody, Timmy is getting it with his nail. But what about Tommy? Oh, Tommy is doing what Timmy is doing, only Tommy only has a spork. Timmy has a nail and Timmy has a spork. But Tommy only has a spork. What does Tommy only have? Tommy only has a spork. See the boys stick the thing with their things? The boys are sticking the thing with their things. But Tommy started sticking it after Timmy started sticking it and Tommy only sticks it the same way Timmy sticks it and Tommy can only stick it only with a spork. If Timmy sticks it this way, then Tommy sticks it this way. If Timmy sticks it that way, then Tommy sticks it that way. Only Tommy can only stick it with a spork. But Bobby, how about Bobby? Is Bobby doing anything at all? What is Bobby doing? Oh, I know, I know. Bobby is talking to himself in his mind. Bobby is saying things to himself in his mind. Bobby is getting ready for him to say something about something. The way Bobby gets ready for him to say something about something is for Bobby first to say it over and over again in his mind. So what is Bobby doing? Can you say what Bobby is doing? Bobby is getting ready for him to say something by practicing saying something over and over again in his mind. Bobby really wants to say things. But Bobby has to get them all set first in his mind. Look, everybody, look! See the thing? Oh, it has lots of colored dots on it and there is stuff all coming out. Who can see the colored dots on it and the stuff all coming out? Ooey, ooey, it's on my spork. Is it on your spork? Ooey, ooey, it got all over my spork. Wait, everybody, wait! Tommy has it all over his spork. Stick out your spork, Bobby. I don't want to stick out my spork. Oh, come on, Bobby, stick out your spork. No. Big baby. Am not, am not! If you're not a baby, then stick out your spork. I don't have to. What a big baby! Stick out your own spork. Oh fuck, what a big baby! I'm telling, I'm telling. Go tell. Who gives a shit if you go tell? Can't we just play? Jesus, fuck, what a big fucking baby! How come you came? Nobody asked you to come. Big stinking fucking baby can't even stick out his spork. Can't make me, can't make me. Who can't make you? You want to see us make you? Wait, wait, the thing, the thing—is the thing getting away? No, no, the thing is not getting away. How could the thing get away? Does anything ever get away? Not one thing in the world ever gets away. Isn't Timmy watching it? Timmy is watching it. Timmy is guarding it. Do you know the word guard? Say the word guard. Let me hear you say the word guard. I love getting it with a spork. This is the best, getting things with a spork. This is how you can really get things with something. Try it like this. Try it with a nail and spork both. This is the best, a nail and a spork both. Now it's bent in two different ways. It's bent up at one dot and bent around at another dot. You know why this is? Who can say why this is? Raise your hand if you can say why this is. It's because it's been getting stuck in its dots. Hey, stick it all of the way down so it's stuck right down through it into the dirt. Oh, hooray, hooray! Now Bobby knows something he can get ready to say. Suppose we listen. Everybody,

everybody, shall we listen to Bobby's mind so we can hear what Bobby is trying to get ready to say? Fellas, fellas, what about we roll him over and see if he's got any of those darn dots of his anywhere on his tummy too. Okay, here is Bobby trying it another way. Guys, guys, let's roll him over and see what the deal is with him underneath. That was Bobby. That was Bobby in his mind getting ready for him to have something to say. Now here's Bobby being Timmy and Tommy in Bobby's mind. A-hole. You hear the a-hole say tummy? Up yours, a-hole. What an a-hole—tummy. Go home, you fucking tummy a-hole jerk. Bobby is such a fucking tummy a-hole jerk. Hey, you fucking tummy a-hole jerk, how would you like it if we take down your pants and look at what's on you underneath? Bobby's hand feels all sticky to him. Do you remember which boy's hand feels all sticky to him? Bobby, it's Bobby, it's Bobby's hand. Bobby is the boy whose hand feels all sticky to him. Mother gets out the meat. Mother gets out the bread. Mother gets out a tiny bottle with white stuff in it. Oh, but wait, wait. Where is the ketchup? Where is the mustard? Where in the name of all that is holy is that fucking jar that had that last little fucking bit of fucking bit of fucking mayo in it? Shall we listen for another little while to what is going on inside of Mother's mind? Songs, there are songs, it is almost all songs that Mother is singing to herself inside of

Mother's mind—such as willow, tit willow, that's one.
Such as the flowers that bloom in the spring, tra la. And
ah, sweet mystery of life, at last I've found thee. And
here comes the one that goes come, come, I love you
only, O come, come, to me. That's the last one, that's the
last. Let's see if you can remember them all. It is time
to see if you remember them all. First, what's first?
Willow, tit willow. Second, what's second? The flowers that bloom in the spring, tra la. And next, say next?
Ah, sweet mystery of life, at last I've found thee. And
last, last? Come, come, I love you only, O come, come,
to me. But what about the boys, the boys? Has Andy
come yet? Has Lew? Who has come to Timmy's yard
to play so far? Can you say who has come to Timmy's
yard for them to play so far? Wait, wait, here is Andy.
Hi, Andy. Hi, missus. Is Lew with you, Andy? Did you
say Lew? Is Lew coming over? Really Lew? All in due
course, Andy, all in due course. May I go play with
Timmy, please? Why of course, Andy, of course. Take
this spork and go look in the yard. Tommy's here. So
is Bobby. All we need now is Lew. Be careful with
your spork. Will you be careful with your spork? Tell
the boys for them to be careful not to poke their eyes
or anything. Can you do that for me, Andy? Yes, missus,
I will. Oh, that's a good boy, Andy. Have a nice time
playing. These sandwiches will all be ready for all of you
in just a jiffy. O the flowers that bloom in the spring,

tra la. O the flowers that bloom in the spring, tra la.
Can you wait for Lew? I can't wait for Lew. Everybody,
hey, everybody, say Lew! Hey, Andy. Hi, Timmy. Hi,
Tommy. Hi, Bobby. Hey, what are you guys doing?
You're not hurting that, are you? Don't hurt that. Let's
just dig, okay? Let's play a game of digging, okay?
Uh-oh, listen, it's Bobby in his mind. I'm turning the
cocksucker over. Get out of the fucking way, you bastards, I'm turning the cocksucker over. Scram, you darn
cocksucking sons of darn bitches, I'm flipping the
cocksucking sonofabitch over. Look how gooey my
spork is, Timmy. You see how gooey my spork is,
Timmy? Who has the gooiest spork, Timmy? Tisk, tisk,
did you hear that, everybody? Shame on Tommy saying
gooiest. All right, everybody, everybody all together
now—shame, shame on Tommy for Tommy saying gooiest. Hey, Timmy, what are you rolling it over for? Did
everybody see Timmy roll it over? Willow, tit willow.
Meat. Bread. A little bit of this and a little bit of that.
Then get the crusts all cut off. Then cut it all in quarters. Oh shit, it's all upside-down now and look at your
spork. Missus, can I have a new spork? I'm busy,
Tommy. Missus, I need another spork. Now, now,
Tommy, didn't I give you a perfectly good spork to begin with? Look at it, missus, please. Now, now,
Tommy—is Tommy going to cry? Oh, Tommy, can't you
see I am busy making everybody lunch? You go back

outside and just be patient. Can't I have that spork? How come can't I have that spork? Oh, Tommy, I am so disappointed in you. That spork is going to be Lew's spork. That spork's Lew's. Oh, missus, mine is all icky, icky, icky. Tommy, Tommy, am I going to have to send you home? Don't you see how nicely the other boys are all playing? Don't you want chocolate milk? Give me this one and Lew can have mine. Why can't Lew have mine? Oh, Tommy, I am so disappointed. How could you be such a disappointment to me? Don't you see how you're wrecking everything? Now look, now look, it sounds like Lew is coming. Is Lew here? Lew, is that you? How come Lew does not answer? Does Lew not know how to answer? Answer, Lew, answer! Here is what Bobby is getting ready to say. Let's listen to what Bobby is getting ready to say. Let's get something else. Squoosh it, squoosh it—then we'll go get something else. Oh, its back, look at its back! Its back is all bent crazy. See how crazy its back is bent? That's from the sporks. Do you know what else it's from? It's also from the nail. Its back is all bent all crazy like that from Timmy and Tommy sticking it in its back with sporks and with a nail. Were we watching when they did it? We were not watching when they did it. But they did it anyway. Did you hear what Andy just said? I'm hungry. Let's play a game of digging a little bit. We could play a game of digging a little bit and then by then we could eat. Get out the chocolate syrup, get out the milk. Ah, sweet mystery of life, at last I've found thee. O come, come, I love you only, come, come, to me. And Bobby, what about him? Bobby's getting ready. Do you hear Bobby getting ready? Let's get Andy, let's get Andy! We're all going to jump you and get you and really do something to you, Andy, if you don't give me your spork. Andy, I'm telling them they better jump you and smash you and beat the shit out of you if you don't give me your spork. Oh, hi, Lew! Yeah, hi, Lew! Did Mother give you a spork? Take a look at what we got over here. You see this, you see this? Get me that fucking rock! Oh, Lew, see how you can dig with a spork? We are going to play a game of digging with our sporks. Who wants to be captain? How about you, Lew? Do you want to be the captain? We were just waiting for you to be captain. Let's review. Shall we review? There is Timmy and there is Tommy and there is Bobby and Andy and who? Who is the last boy? Is it Lew? Yes, yes, the last boy is Lew. It is Lew who is littlest and last—so this would be one of the reasons among all the unrevealed reasons for us to watch out for Lew. Because Lew is littlest and last. Go get me that fucking rock! Could I borrow your spork, Lew, could I? Ass-wipe! Bunch of sissy ass-wipes! Take this plastic shit and get me the fucking rock! Come, come, I love you only, come, come, to me. Who wants to see how gooey it can get? You want to see how gooey it can get? Look at them. See them things with them wings over there? And ants. Hey, how about we let us get some ants? Let's spork the shit out of a whole bunch of ants! The flowers that bloom in the spring, tra la, the flowers that bloom in the spring. Can't count any dots now, can you? Hand me the nail. It's my nail. Give me the nail. It's my yard and my nail. Can't we just play digging? Selfish little prick. I'll give it back. Give it here for a sec and I'll give it right back. It's his, it's his. Shut your face. Make him shut his face, Lew. Lew, I'd like to see you make him do it, Lew. Shut his yap for him. Shut his hole. Shut your hole! Willow, tit willow. Oh, everybody, look—here comes Mother with everything on a platter all ready for everybody to eat. Dive in, boys. Get ready to dive in. Ah, sweet mystery of life, at last I've found thee. Ah, I know at last the secret of it all. Guys, guys, there is this great idea I've got which I have been thinking about. Hey, guys, no kidding around—don't you guys want to hear this great idea? It's spork-collection time. Mother, Mother, collecting all sporks! Each boy will wipe off his spork on his sandwich, face me and drop his spork at his feet. Stick the bitch, stick her! No, no, stick anything instead. What instead? There's never any instead. Come, come, I love you only, come, come, to me. Answer me, answer me. Isn't answerability everything, Lew? Everybody,

everybody, tell Lew. Is not answerability not the very
thing of everything, Lew? Ah, sweet mystery of life, at
last I've found thee. Foon the bitch before she sporks
us all to hell. But she did not have to. Mother did not
have to. Remember the white stuff? Oh, come on,
don't say you don't remember the white stuff! All right,
here's a new one. Is a spork a foon, or a foon a spork?
Raise your hand if you need extra help. A spork is not
a foon because a foon is what? Gee willikers, class, see
the white stuff go to work on them all? Anybody, anybody, come take a seat down in front if you cannot see
the secret of it all.

MAN ON THE GO

I DON'T KNOW, YOU FIGURE IT OUT. All I know is I am not a spiteful person. At least not to my own mind I am not. A spiteful person, that is. Or maybe spiteful is not the exact idea of the thing. Maybe mean is closer to the idea of the thing as far as the spirit of it goes. Besides, why would I want to be mean to my wife? She was as nice a person as anybody could ask for. Which is another thing. Why would God come take her away from me when she was such a nice person? Go ahead and answer me that one, if you please. Anyway, it's all totally confusing to me, God's behavior as far as this thing goes. The point is, the wife's gone, is the thing, and I am where? I am here, is where I am. I am right here in the same place which the two of us used to be in, except now I am in it alone with just me and the washing machine and the other things, okay? Hey, it's a terrific washing machine. I am not for one minute saying it's not. The wife picked it out and nobody could take care of a job like picking something out better than the wife could. The wife was a whiz at all of that. She'd get these pamphlet things and these booklet things the companies put out and all night from night to night the wife would read up on it all about it and then she'd make what is known in the trade as the decision of an educated consumer. I'm telling you, the wife knew her onions forwards and backwards when it came to your home appliances. And the washing machine, I would have to say this washing machine was one of the wife's more outstanding selections. Talk about your service. This thing really comes across with the service. It's got the stamina and it's got the endurance. Hell, it's got performance up the wazoo, is what it's got, and that's no joke. Hey, who hasn't been wised up as to how these companies are always sitting there where they make these things like washing machines making them so there's down inside them like this death thing which they've built into them so the thing will just all of a sudden go ahead and rear up on you when it's been told and crap the hell out on you and leave you high and dry? I know the deal. You know the deal. Who doesn't know the deal is to get everybody to dig down in their wallet and go get themselves a new one to come in there and take the place of the dead one? Please, let us not kid ourselves as to what the score really is, even if, speaking economy-wise, they say it is all in the end for the best as far as it being in the best interests of everybody in the end, speaking consumer-wise as far as the economy. Fine. I am not arguing against it. I am not setting myself up as any expert against it. All I am saying is you couldn't pin a thing about anything like that on this baby which the wife got. It's a pip. You know what a pip is? It's a pip, which you can take my word for it, is the exception which broke the rule. And don't think I don't know it would probably be a hex on it for

me to tell you how old this honey is. It would knock
you right back on your heels for you to hear how many
a year this honey has been operating for this household
without a hitch as far as what is referred to as your daily
operation—up until, fuck it, damn it, this morning.
Which brings me back to spiteful—am I spiteful, or full
of spite? Unless the crux of the thing is meanness
which is at the bottom of it. Because what happens this
morning is the fucking thing this morning, it starts
screeching all over on me, wobbling and squealing and
smoking and carrying on like the fucking thing is going to go totally nuts on me. I am serious. Hey, there
is this, Jesus Christ, there's this, you call it, a catastrophe
which is commencing to blow up the fuck all over on
me. I'm telling you, all hell is busting loose. Shit, I as
the sole resident in charge did not know if I am supposed to phone the people that run the insane asylum
or the firemen. The thing is just going into its what the
brochure has got the gall to stand there and tell you is
its agitation cycle, when goodbye and good luck, it's
fucking all of a sudden like sobbing out its heart at you
and everything. I go fill this bucket and hit the thing
with this broomstick I got to get the switch on it
switched off. Hey, I was scared out of my fucking mind,
let me tell you. Look at me, look at me, I am trembling
from stem to stern, if you really want to know what was
going on on the premises here. Shit, I am standing there

waiting for the thing to come get me, is how I honestly as a human being felt in the situation. Okay, I overloaded it, case closed. I am not going to sit here and try to prevaricate to anybody about it. One thing about my nature, it's the truest thing about my nature, don't expect to ever catch me going around shying away from the facts and shirking them like your average man on the street does. Believe you me, one thing I am not like is like the Lord sitting up there and going ahead and taking a person's wife away from them and then, when they get their nerve worked up and ask Him about it, He stands there and hands them all this bullshit from the bible and so on. I come clean with people. If it's a bitter pill, I am the first one to walk right up to it and swallow it. I don't flinch. I don't look for excuses. I face the music and take my medicine. This is why I am so completely prepared to sit down and go over it with you and let the facts come out where there is no help for it but that they have to, whereas meanwhile the fucking chips can fucking fall where they may. To come totally clean with you, this is where individuals such as you and me have to take ourselves in hand and go over the idea of am I spiteful as a human being or mean. Because overloading the thing, because not under any circumstances ever overloading the thing, because take it or leave it, this was the wife's first and last word on the subject of the washing machine. Well, okay, you hear me not admitting it? I overloaded. As far as the various trials and tribulations, sue me, I overloaded. Hey, the wife was hardly in her grave when, go know, I could not as far as the facts stop myself from overloading. This is where the whole policy of me always sticking the broomstick next to the washing machine comes in. For tamping. For ramming. For getting the stuff packed in. Oh, the wife was always saying you overload, you over-tax. This is what the wife used to say. The wife used to say not only do you overtax, not only are you over-taxing, but you as the consumer are opening the flood-gates for scum to come up in there and build up in the pipes on you and wreck the whole fucking deal. This was one of the biggest things with the wife—start with the right appliance and treat it right right from the start. Otherwise, you get scum. Otherwise, scum starts rush-ing in at you through the floodgates and it goes and gets itself set up against you and then, buddy boy, then you got trouble. So be it. I went ahead and did it—so, hey, it went ahead and did it, didn't it? Oh, it's one thing for you to be all set with a bucket. I was all set to swing into action with the bucket. But forget it. The thing quit making all that rumpus when I got it with the broomstick and cut it off. No question about it, there's enough smoke out there for you to choke a horse out there, but we can relax about getting the firemen or the cops to come over or anybody from the loony bin.

The flames and all that, it all, as far as one of your emergencies which gets out of control, it's all blown over as far as that. Tell you what. You want to know what? Because it could be it's high time I quit working the toilet handle so hard too. Don't worry, the wife didn't not give me all the lowdown you could use as far as that topic itself. Hand to God, she warned me, didn't she? The wife said things can't take a thing like that. The wife said the thing with people is them always putting too much rough stuff on things. Her philosophy was take care of them. Her philosophy was respect them. Her philosophy was use your natural intelligence on them when you have to go and deal with them and no, nobody in your house will be sorry and neither will the household budget. Easy does it was the by-word of the wife. That was it in a nutshell—easy does it, darn it, Gordo. The thing is, I was squinching too much stuff down in it, wasn't I? That's the whole story as far as the long and short of it, squinching too much down. Fuck it. I am probably moving out. They've got these laundries where you can go, don't you know. Since when does a man on the go need anything like a whole washing machine just for himself? And what's so wrong with a public toilet, I'd like to know? Tell me what is so unhuman and horrible as far as your public toilet in America? Sure, no one is stopping me from calling the toilet and washing machine companies for me to see what the bastards have to say. But won't they just stand there and ask me what the piss is wrong with me, didn't you never learn for you not to go back on your wife? Hell, when don't you know what people are going to say to you before the son of a bitches say it? Am I interested in these companies? I am not interested in those companies. I am all for America and I am all for the economy, but those dirty rats just want to say what they want to say behind your fucking back. Name me anybody which just can't wait to think the worst. You couldn't do it, could you? Do I as a customer have to sit here and live the rest of my life taking all that guff off all them bums like that? Hey, you can count on it, I am definitely moving the first chance I get. Get out of here, is the thing. One thing I might take, maybe the one fucking thing I might take, it's probably going to be the broomstick in case the Lord makes me have to keep on dealing with any more of your average people. Or does a thing like saying this sound to you like the individual which said it is crawling all over with spiteful intentions? Big deal. I care a lot what you think. Oh, I am scared to death what you think. Oh, I am shaking in my boots what somebody such as you happens to think. You want to talk about spite and malice, how about we decide to make up our minds to begin with Him? Or meanness, if meanness is your thing. You want to see somebody get the hell out of somewhere, keep your eye on this individual here. Unless you think they made it, when they made it, with some burning time in it built into it. But then there's the toilet handle, isn't there? And the chairs and the tables and the walls and the sink. Listen, there comes a time when, face it, the party's over. Your household scum building up on you isn't the only thing. Whatever the companies do or don't do, forget it, what's it anymore to me? It is like there's this newborn running to the graveyard hollering its head off at everybody, screaming like a maniac at them I can't go, I can't go. You know what they stand there and say to you? Because they stand there and say to you hey, please—even at your age age-wise, pay attention, you already went already.

ORIGINS OF DEATH

SHE CALLS ME AND SHE SAYS TO ME hey there's three words I hate, so I says to her yeah sure there are three words you hate, and so she says to me you want to know what they are, and so I says to her yeah sure tell me what they are, I want to know me what they are, and so she says to me sty, one of them is sty, and so I says to her which sty, and so she says to me what do you mean which sty, she says to me I said sty so what do you mean which sty, so I says to her well there's the sty you get in your eye and there's the other one, there's the pig one, oh she says to me, oh the pig one she says to me, I wasn't thinking of the pig one she says to me, it's the eye one which I was thinking of says she to me, so I says to her so which one do you hate more, the pig one or the eye one, and so she says to me can I call you back, and I so I says to her sure call me back so go ahead and call me back and so she calls me back and she says to me I don't know what got into me thinking I needed to think about it, why did I have to think about it, there is no reason for me to have to think about it, it's the eye sty, it's the sty in the eye one, the sty in the eye one is the sty I hate, but what about the other one says I to her, how do you feel about the other one, the pig one, how do you feel about the pig one, don't you as a word hate the pig one as a word, well says she to me as a word I never thought about the pig one as a word, you want for me to start thinking about the pig one as a word, I'm going to have to hang up and call you back about it after I have thought about it as far as the pig one that way as a word, no I says, I says to her no, don't get yourself upset about this subject anymore says I to her it's enough for me to know you wanted me to know something you hate, it makes me feel a lot closer to you hearing you tell me about a word which you really feel you hate, but what about the other two says I to her, the other two what says she to me, what do you mean the other two says she to me, the words says I to her, what words says she to me, the three words you're saying to me you hate, don't you remember calling me telling me there's three words you really feel you really hate, oh she says yeah I did she says, that's definitely right she says, thanks for reminding me she says, so what are they says I to her, what are they says I to her, I forgot she says to me, I can't think of them anymore says she to me, so I says to her maybe you were just trying to impress me, maybe when you said three to me all you were trying to do with me was just to impress me when you said that to me, maybe the thing of it when you said it was you felt saying it was just the one word would not im-press me as much as saying it to me it was three words, maybe says I to her, maybe you never had any three words you hated to begin with says I to her, so I says to her don't worry about the other two, I'm plenty im-pressed with just the one word you already told me all about, okay can I change the subject with you she says to me, sure I says to her change the subject with me if you want to change the subject with me I says to her, it's okay with me if you change the subject with me says I to her, the bags she says, the bags I says, the bags she says, the bags they give you when you go get your stuff at the market she says to me you know those bags she says to me, you know those bags like tissue paper she says to me, they're these shitty plastic bags that are like tissue paper she says to me, okay I says to her, I'm with you all the way I says to her, shoot I says to her, the subject is the shitty bags they give you says I myself to her, the ones that are like this tissue paper shit says she to me, from the market says she to me, okay I says, okay the bags from the market I says, they used to give you like real paper bags she says to me, you remember when they used to give you like these nice brown paper bags says she to me, but now look, she says, now look, be-cause do they give you real bags like that anymore, be-cause they don't give you real bags like that anymore, now you go to the market and they give you what, be-cause they give you like these next-to-nothing things that are like shit says she to me, so okay I says to her so now they give you these lousy things instead of giving you the real things, so what about it says I to her, so what about what says she to me, whereupon I says about the crappy bags they give you, what about the crappy bags they give you, you were saying they used to give everybody these great old regular paper ones and now they give you these shitty flimsy crappy ones, well they do says she they absolutely do and like I was just thinking the nerve of these fucking people, where do they get their nerve, these fucking people, you used to walk out of the store and you had a real bag at least, now what do you have, now you don't even have anything you can fold and put away and save anymore, these crappy flimsy shitty things they give you, you can't fold them and put them away like a regular bag anymore, ball them up says I to her, ball them up she says to me, yeah you ball them up and stuff them in a bag and save them that way says I to her, that's what you do she says to me you ball them up and stuff them in a bag and keep them that way she says to me, yeah sure I says to her that's what I do I says to her, you say you ball them up and stuff them in a bag and save them she says to me I never saw you ball them up and stuff them in any fucking bag she says to me, well I do says I, I do it all the time says I, oh so you do says she to me I don't believe it she says to me, you ball them up and stuff them in a bag she says to me, check I says that's what I do I says, really she says, really I says, so are you being sarcastic with me she says, because I don't like it if you're being sarcastic with me says she to me, come over and look for yourself I says, I can't go out she says I got a sty in my eye she says, I'm sorry I says, that's okay she says just don't start getting sarcastic with me she says, I can take a lot from people she says but people being sarcastic with me is one thing I can't take from people, okay I says to her I'm sorry about your sty I says to her, she says forget it she says it won't kill me she says all I want you to know is if there's three things I can't take it's definitely sarcasm which is one of them, okay I says I'll remember that I says, don't forget it she says, check I says I'll remember it I says, so she says to me don't you want to know what the other two ones are, yeah sure I says to her tell me what the other two ones are, she says okay so I told you sarcasm is one of them, somebody sassing me is another one of them, and anybody teasing me is the third one of them, so is that impressive enough for you or what says she to me, hey I'm impressed I says to her, I promise you I am definitely impressed I says to her, well make sure you are says she to me and another thing she says, what I says, tell me what I says, what's the other thing I says.

UNDER A PEDIMENT

In the beginning was schizophrenia.

—GILLES DELEUZE

IT WAS THE NOTES I was getting. I was getting these notes. I was developing this terrific collection of really great notes. Normally the thing of it with me is I just go ahead. I get a title and I just go ahead. But this was a case where there were all of these great notes I was developing and where they just kept on accumulating on me and accumulating, is the only way for anybody with any intelligence to put it. The other thing is a title, the title. Didn't have one, couldn't get one. Nothing. Then out of the blue I hear myself saying to myself wait a minute, wait a minute, under a pediment, how about under a pediment? Except first I had to go over to the museum and ask one of the people. They have these guards over there. These attendants, personnel in uniform. So there's this one of them who says to me yeah, that's right, pediment, the name of it you call it is a pediment. So this is when I had the whole thing. I was all set when I had this last part of the thing, which, considering my history, my history considered, is for me the same as the staples of the thing—i.e., a title; viz., a title, get a title, then go ahead and write your head off now that you have got it, the title. But so who ever had any notes before? I never had any notes before. Notes for me never were this regular thing for me. Notes is such a crazy new thing for me. But so what happens was it turns around and gets captivating to me. As a separate thing to me. Notes, getting notes. It's like you might say these notes I was collecting, they were evolving into this thing which was evolving into its own kind of a thing non-relative to anything. Talk about notes. I'm telling you, if anybody wants to see tons of them, then they better come see me about it because I am the one with tons of them. But so how does this happen to come about? Does anybody have any idea of how this happens to come about? Because until we as a society can get to the bottom of this thing and start making some progress rooting it out or getting it rooted out, the human race will just go on being enslaved as a nation in bondage. Meanwhile, stay alert. Keep your guard up. The snare is everywhere. The only way for us as a people to come to terms with this is for you and other enlightened citizens to continue to see to it that you have kept yourselves informed, unclogged the lines of communication, and to have made wariness—wariness!— your watchword. Because it's first it's this thing and then it's next this next thing and then that's it—it's, you know, it's everything everywhere.

But a bird does not say to itself okay, here goes a feather, I am finished with this feather, I am getting rid of this feather. Because the man was prepared to believe no bird relieved itself of a feather in hopes the man would retrieve it. There was not a matter of mind to be inquired into. Although neither was it an accident, was it? Nothing was an accident. A scheme was bound to be bound up in it, whatever it was, somewhere. For example, hadn't the man once been in the company of a boy who said feder for feather? This is what the man pondered about, or pondered on, thinking ponderingly, "What's the deal?"

The man reasoned along this line, or bethought himself along this line of reasoning. For did it not stand to reason that not everyone in the present dispensation could report of himself his once having been in the company of a boy who said feder for feather? Wasn't there something going on in this somewhere, and couldn't you end up somewhere in it dying from it? There were hints, there were foretokenings—the proof was everywhere for anyone with the acumen to read the dread indications. There would be a disease conducted into the man from this relation he had conceived with the feathers. It would be a feather-borne disease, despite the care the man took never to handle a feather directly. No, no, this last, that last sentence, all wrong, it's all too wrong—wrought, wrought, it's all too wrong and wrought, diction thick with effort. I can't write this. It cannot be written.

But, oh, the thrill of them!

Feathers.

The abundance.

The very copia.

Now that the man had started noticing.

Mustn't it mean these birds were everywhere?

Or had been?

Although there were times when the man could go from the bottom of the city to the top of it and not spot the first feather. But around in front of the museum, this was where there were always to be found good pickings. On the other hand, the man could not always take himself to the museum, could he? It was not always convenient for the man to go to the museum. You did not get to the museum by going in the direction the man was mainly given to going in, which instead was the direction of the market.

The market.

Here was where the man got his groceries, earlier called to your attention by the noun staples.

And, oh, the cleaning materials!

Kaptain Kleeno, for instance.

The direction that took the man to the market, this was the direction the man was given to walking in, whereas the museum was opposite of this, and rather a longer walk by half. Forget it. I'm worn out with this. I'm disgusted with this. I am absolutely exhausted with this and am anyway stalled in my tracks with this. Mind is elsewhere. You know what it is to stand under a pediment? He did not know where the feathers came from. He did not care to know where it was on the body of the birds the feathers came from, or had come from.

From wing, from tail, from under the gut, it all sickened the man. Expressions of life sickened the man. The man seemed excited as much for the thing they were known by as for the thing they were.

But how say which is which?—feather here, feather there. Feder. Later on in this it will be said to the man, someone will later on in this come to say to the man, "You feather your nest? This your game, you feather your nest?" Was the bleach killing him? The man was convinced the bleach could be killing him. Or the ammonia. Forget Kaptain Kleeno. Scratch Kaptain Kleeno. No one's buying it, no one's falling for it, something named by the name Kaptain Kleeno. But couldn't anything kill a person? Everything could kill a person. The least little thing could kill anybody—and would. This sentence, for instance. Even just the comma in it.

Ever think of collecting the names of soaps?

Palmolive?

Woodbury?

Camay?

Pears, Dove, Castile?

How could you say something wasn't killing you if it were doing it in increments too small for you to tell?

Isn't this why they say imperceptibly?

An ant might know, on the one hand, or a tortoise on the other.

But not a man.

Aren't there mites on feathers?

He soaked them in a solution of his making.

The man mixed ammonia and bleach and bleach and ammonia.

And Kaptain Kleeno.

Used the tweezers to deliver the day's gatherings to the basin where the purifications were done. It was a plastic basin, bought for the very thing, and disposed of and replaced every several days, for fear a swarm of undead mites might have come to congregate in it, having furiously replenished themselves in a crevice where traces of moisture would coalesce into a natal soup too teensy to be detected without special optics.

I suppose you know where it was the man got his plastic basins from. Well, it was in that direction that the man so often pointed himself. Counter-museum-ward, that is. Ivory Soap, Lux Soap, Murphy's in a pinch. Not that results were not also to be had along the old wall along the way to either destination, a rumply mossy affair of mortar and stone declaring the great wilderness to its one side and the city to its other. Ah, the man had heard them in there, the rats in there. Had heard them jostling around in there, disturbing the loose earth with their wormy hairy tails. There were times when a wind could make the man weep. There were times when the man might have fallen to his knees in grief for the wind that had rushed forth from its lair and reached from him the feather he was about to take. The man never took a feather with his fingers. It was unthinkable, unthinkable! This was why the man was dying, wasn't it?

His precautions, the tweezers, the ablutions in the basin, didn't the man choose death from care over death from disease? Someone said something once. Hadn't someone once said something once? Liver fluke, a liver fluke, this is what the man thought he remembered someone once saying once—touch a feather with your finger and get a liver fluke. But what would it be, a liver fluke? The man stood over the basin with the magnifying glass and tweezers.

The fumes were impossible. That plural or singular? The feather lay bathing on the one side. It would be necessary to catch it by the spine and reverse it onto its other side. You call it rachis, I call it spine. The source for liver fluke, was it the same as that for "You feather your nest? This is your game, you feather your nest?" I can't stand this anymore. I am so totally fed up with this and with everything else evermore. Wait a minute, so wait a minute—so how come the man didn't write this in French? He is trying to break the habit. What if I leave the city? What if I just get everything I've got and just leave? The man did not know how they lost a feather—was it from sickness or from combat or age? There was once this time once when I was walked right up to by a robber once and I said to him the money take the money but can't I keep these? I keep them in a thing which used to have bits of matchbooks in it and when I get the top off to get another one in, they make a noise like shhhhhhhhhhhhhhhhhhhhhhhhhh. It's terrible, it's terrible—shhhhhhhhhhhhhhhhhhhhhhhhh. How did it start? Does anyone know how it starts? Here's the thing—shhhhhhhhhhhhhhhhhhhhhhhh.

Yardley.

Tide.

Duz.

Era.

Dial.

Cheer.

Wisk.

Joy.

Dawn.

Oh yes, of course—"You feather your nest? This is your game, you feather your nest?"

Shhhhhhhhhhhhhhhhhhhhhhhhh.

Cark, cark—what does cark mean?

Fella says everything in depth is horrible.

Fella says the sensibility that reaches out for the sense in things makes contact with the impossibility in them.

Yes, he was feathering it.

This was the whole idea of it—to feather it, to get it feathered, to make certain there were feathers in it.

Finland is a gaudy-feathered place.

Could I ask you a personal question?

Why am I sitting here making every excuse for you?

I used to think polio in Italy meant impetigo.

Or vice versa.

Ivory Scales.

Ivory Sleet.

Caress.

The man took to walking.

The man walked everywhere and took everything—
the remains of matchbooks, the names of soaps—
shhhhhhhhhhhhhhhhhhhhh—notes, feathers.

Here's the thing.

Feder when I was a child.

You got the thing?

That's the thing.

Look no word in the eye.

Or the mouth.

Except pediment.

Except for pediment.

HOW THE SOPHIST GOT SPOTTED

I'M SUING.
Who are you suing?
Wouldn't you like to know.
Are you suing me?
You'll find out.

I'm suing.
Who are you suing?
Somebody. People.
Which people?
Just people.

I'm suing.
Who are you suing?
Just some people.
Do I know them?
Ask me no questions, I'll tell you no lies.

I'm suing.
Who are you suing?
That's for me to know.
How come you can't tell me?
Oh, how come I can't tell you.

I'm suing.
Why are you suing?
Have to. No choice.

Can't you work it out?

Work what out?

What you're suing over.

Who told you I'm suing?

You did.

I said I'm suing?

Two seconds ago.

Well, I am. I'm suing.

So what about?

Things.

What things?

Things they did.

Irreparable things?

Intolerable things.

Think it over first.

I thought already.

Suing's a big step.

That's why I'm taking it.

You have a lawyer?

I'll get a lawyer.

You need a good lawyer.

I'll get a good lawyer.

They cost, you know.

I look like I just got off the boat?

Talk about bucks per hour, oh boy!

I look like I'm still wet behind the ears?

Guess what a lawyer gets.

I look like I'm just a babe in the woods?
Show me a lawyer on welfare.
I look like I haven't been around the block?
Just watch yourself, is all I'm saying.
I look like I was born yesterday?
Just watch your step.
You see me in diapers?
I'm just saying.

I'm suing.
Why do you want to sue?
Bring the bastards to their knees.
Which bastards?
Oh, wouldn't you like to know.

I'm suing.
Better watch it.
Watch what?
Suing somebody.
Why should I worry about suing somebody?
They could sue back.
They could sue back?
Countersue.
Countersue for what?
For suing.
People can do that?
Anybody can do that.

The bastards. The dirty rotten crummy bastards.

I'm suing.
Why sue? Mediate instead.
Mediate?
Come to terms.
What terms?
Give a little, take a little.
Don't sue?
Don't sue.
But there are issues involved.
Issues, shmissues.
It's people like you.
It's people like me what?
It's people like you.
It's people like me what?
You know.

I'm suing.
So you're suing.
I'm really going to sue.
It's your right.
I'm within my rights.
It's permitted under law.
It's the remedy under the law.
People can sue.
Oh, don't I know it.

So who's the defendant?

Can't discuss it.

You can't discuss it?

Can't discuss it.

But why'd you tell me in the first place?

Tell you what? Who told you anything?

You told me you're going to sue.

That's right. Can't wait, either.

You want my advice?

What's your advice?

Make a deal. Don't sue.

No deals. I don't make deals.

Think it over.

Thought it over plenty already.

Just promise me you'll think it over.

Justice, sweetheart, you never heard of justice?

Justice for who?

For the one in the right.

Who's that?

I'm that.

Are you suing me?

No comment.

Are you suing me?

My lips are sealed.

It's me you're suing, isn't it?

Does the shoe fit?

But why are you suing me?

Who said it's you?

Just don't forget, boyo.

Just don't forget what?

Two can play the same game.

What game is that?

The suing game.

I say I'm suing someone?

You think I can't take a hint?

Who hinted? I didn't hint.

So sue me if you're going to sue me.

What's the hurry? I'm in no hurry.

What about we talk it out?

I'm through with talking.

I can make concessions.

Name me a couple.

I could give ground.

Describe the ground.

There are areas.

I'm listening. Tell me areas.

I need time.

An honest person needs time?

Recoup, regroup. Think straight.

I'll settle for one area.

Would you take an apology?

It depends. I'll ask my lawyer.

I'm prepared to make steep concessions.

I like that. How steep?

You won't be sorry.

That's up to my lawyer.

Can't we keep the lawyers out of this?

Innocent people don't plead.

Be reasonable. I wasn't ready for this.

Ready for what?

For bringing a lawsuit.

You're suing? Who are you suing?

It's a countersuit.

You don't say.

They sue you, you sue them.

Tit for tat?

Tit for tat.

This is your last word in the matter?

You just heard it.

Which is it, tit or tat?

You see why everybody wants to sue you?

Who wants to sue me?

Everybody does.

For asking a question?

For irking people.

I just remembered.

What did you just remember?

Who I'm suing. I'm suing people.

What have people ever done to you?

Did I just go crazy?

What have people ever done to you?

Am I out of my mind?

What have people ever done to you?

Excuse me, but did I just now go out of my mind?

I'm only asking.

You want what? You want names and addresses?

I'll take a name. Also an address.

This is why I am suing you.

You're suing me?

Now you know why I'm suing you.

So sue me. I'm filing a countersuit.

Good.

We'll sue each other.

Good.

We'll sue one another.

Good.

This'll resolve it for good.

Good.

Are you mocking me?

You bastard. I'll fix you. I'll finish you.

You were always against me, weren't you?

You'll pay through the nose.

We'll see who pays.

Monkey see, monkey do.

You'll sing a different tune.

Oh, I'm trembling. See me tremble?

You'll all pay. Every last one of you.

Have you seen a doctor?

I can't wait. I just can't wait.

See a doctor.

Don't worry, we'll see who's crazy.

Consult a doctor. It's for the best.

You swine will stop at nothing.

I feel sorry for you.

Shame, for shame. How can you stand yourself?

You are really a very sick human being.

I'm sick, I'm sick. We'll see who's sick.

There but for the grace of God and so forth.

You give thanks? I give thanks.

This is a perfect example.

Example of what, example of what?

Don't you see yourself? Take a look at yourself.

Me? Take a look at me?

It's sad. It's really sad.

That's some joke, you saying sad.

You're confused, aren't you?

Who's confused? I'm supposed to be confused?

Good God, you don't know who's who or what's what.

Who doesn't know? I don't know?

All you can do is mimic me, can't you?

You're gaslighting me, aren't you?

You know the word nuts?

This is a gaslighting thing, isn't it?

Is that a movie reference, gaslighting?

You're trying to throw me off.

We worry for you. We're trying to help you.

That's so low. That's the lowest.

There's cause for concern.

You'd stoop to a saying.

I'm just saying.

You'd stoop to an alliteration.

Everyone's concerned.

You'd get down and wallow with a cliche.

We have your best interest at heart.

I could vomit from this.

Are you all right?

I could really throw up from this.

Do you want to sit down?

This is too much.

Lie down for a bit.

No dice.

Take some time out for a bit.

Nothing doing.

You can sue later.

I'm suing now.

Can't it wait?

What do you take me for?

Rest a while.

You take me for a fool, don't you?

Give things a chance to work themselves out.

Things worsen. Everything worsens.

Oh so true. But suing's not the answer.

It couldn't hurt. And I'll feel better.

That's what we want, isn't it?

Isn't what?

For you to feel better.

I'd like to feel better.

Of course you would.

I'd really like to.

And you shall, you shall.

You're humoring me.

Who's humoring you?

This is disgusting. People are disgusting.

Calm yourself.

I wouldn't give you the satisfaction.

Why make a mountain out of a molehill?

Filth.

Please.

You filth.

No need, there's no need.

I'll show you need.

Just hang on a little longer.

You want hang? I'll give you hang.

You're upset.

How dare you talk to me like this.

So sue us.

Us? Where's us?

Just a manner of speaking. Lie down.

Skip it.

Just for two seconds lie down.

Forget it.

Here. Lie here.

No.

You know you want to.

No.

Oh now, you know you do.

What for?

To feel better. To feel good.

I'd like to feel good.

Of course you would. Who wouldn't?

Just for a minute.

That's right.

I'm tired.

How could you not be?

I'm so tired.

We're all of us weary through and through.

Why is that?

It's tiring.

Truer words were never etc.

There's the proof.

There's what?

The proof.

What proof?

Etc. You said etc.

The rest of it would have killed me.

My meaning exactly.

I'd never have made it.

The syllables. It's never not the syllables.

We're perishing from the syllables.

Why is it, why is it?

Do the math.

The divisor is?

Syllables, number of.

And the dividend?

Oh, Jesus.

What's the dividend?

It's, oh, it's a certain variable.

Variable how?

Who can say? Can anyone say?

But is it known?

Try one. Try an infinitely divisible one.

Cut it out. Infinition?

Try it.

Head's spinning.

Lie down.

Don't feel so hot.

Who does?

Really feeling pretty lousy.

Let's get those shoes off.

Feel bad. Honest.

Me too.

All the phonemes, Christ.

Don't forget the hyphens. Even just the periods.

You're saying don't speak.

I'm just saying.

But you're saying don't speak.

Touch.

Touch instead?

Just touch.

Touch divided into the time you've got?

Touches.

But supposing, just supposing.

Go ahead and suppose.

Well, what gets done?

One lives.

But in the way of things.

My very meaning.

Touch?

And be touched.

But this, all this, isn't it speech?

Shh.

Don't speak?

Shh.

Don't sue?

Shh.

Just shush?

Hush.

Nothing but this?

What is there but this?

I'm getting everything off.

Yes.

It's all coming off.

Yes.

Once I get going, don't look for me to quit.

Yes.

Now's the time.

Yes.

Now's the only time.

That's it.

It's all contracting.

Um.

It's all condensing.

Isn't it?

It all comes down to only this.

No, no—not this—that.

That?

Yes, that.

You never said that.

What else but that?

But you said this.

I said this?

I swear you said this.

But this is that.

This is that?

You think not?

It's what anyone thinks—this and that.

It? Which it is it that is that it?

You're gaslighting me again.

This is the movie, you mean.

Gaslight me one more time.

And you'll do what?

I'll sue.

So sue.

I'm suing.

You're suing me?

I'm suing you.

So everything up to this point was pointless?

But look how far we got.

I tried to save you.

Thanks for that.

This is the thanks I get for that?

That's the thanks you get for this.

Got.

See why I'm suing?

But why sue me? Sue how we speak.

You see that? Do you see it, do you see it?

See what?

Sue at the beginning of a sentence.

This was to see sue at the beginning of a sentence?

Not this, but that.

All that was just to see sue like that?

You want my answer?

You owe me an answer.

The answer is it wasn't until it was.

Thou art not August unless I make thee so.

—WALLACE STEVENS